SMOKE GHOST

by

Ghazwan Saaid

ISIS AND THE SMOKE GHOST

by

Ghazwan Saaid

Paley, Whately Greenleaf Press

ISIS and the Smoke Ghost
by Ghazwan Saaid

Published by
Paley, Whately, and Greenleaf Press
An Imprint of *Athanatos Publishing Group*

ISBN: 978-1-936830-97-8

Website: www.thesmokeghost.com

And the LORD God planted a garden eastward in Eden; and there he put the man whom he had formed.

Genesis.

"When everything starts to accumulate and you reach to the point where you can't endure any more, be aware, not to give up or surrender. As at this point your destiny will be changed"

Mawlana Jalal Al-din Al- Rumy, a 13th-century Muslim Sofi.

He started his trip with a bag, full of his obsessions and tangled thoughts, storming through his head on occasions and making his life more difficult than normal. It was not coincidence that drove him to this point. He was sure of that. There were exceptional circumstances and crucial factors, working together over many years, leading to where he is now.

He inhaled deeply from his cigarette which he rarely dropped from his fingers. He exhaled, meditating in the various shapes that the smoke formed around him. Having spent all his life alone, without a companion, the cigarette became a body, sharing his life of misery with him.

For him, the cigarette was like a partner, a woman that he missed and could never have. He would touch it gently with his fingers, feeling its delicate smoothness, testing it between his lips with lust. He watched its flame glow, feeling the warmth it emitted. It gave life to his cold world. Its smells and scents going deep into his weak body, he never left it, even when he was in bed at night. Simply put, he replaced everything he had lost in his life because of odd thoughts about wrapped tobacco in white paper. The cigarette was the only outlet that made his hard lonely life bearable. Its magical smoke surrounded him, no longer knowing where to lay his head.

He moved his hand down; touching the bag to make sure it was still there. The trip he made days ago was a real fact, not just a dream. One question was spinning around in his head as he sat in the chair on the street corner, drinking his tea: is it worth it? All the things that he had lost; all of the sacrifices that he made for this trip. All that time he spent and all of his hard work, causing deep insight into his soul. He was comparing it with all the years of his life he had spent searching for something different, something new, during his long quest to be a different person.

He rejected all that he had in his community, everybody around him, mostly his people. He hated the language that he used to speak with them. The only language he knew in his life. Specifically, when he joined them in prayer, repeating the same words, without knowing what these words were supposed to mean. It didn't make any sense to him, all these movements of bowing, standing and hands moving. What kind of religion was he professing? How can he worship a God that sends people to hell if they don't fear him?!

He refused to be one of them and wanted to be a different person. But now, after this hard journey, he doesn't know why he feels like a stranger, not only to his people and family but, also to himself. He became incapable of understanding what he wanted. This is possibly one of the reasons he was far away from his family.

Expelling the smoke out of his mouth, the image of his father appeared among the foggy pictures in front of him. His father was whispering to his mother:

"I don't understand! Our son Salah is confusing me."

"What do you mean" the mother said? She dropped what she had in her hands, paying full attention.

"I know he is different from his brother, but the new things and thoughts in his life, I just have some concerns."

"What new things?" She became more worried.

"Don't you know? Your son is attending the church but, I don't know what he is up to now."

The mother was stunned for a while. She then replied with panic; "Oh God help us! He is not going to become a Christian. What shall we do? What shall we tell the people if this is true? What shame we will bring to our family."

The father replied disturbed: "What are you talking about? I know my son very well. Maybe he is different in some parts of his life from the other young men his age, but he is still a man with sense. He knows that there are certain lines people can't cross. We can't change. This is the law of life."

His mother and father were ordinary citizens, spending their life trying to take care of their children. They protected them, doing their best to be good parents for their five children. However, they had lost two of their sons while Salah was a young boy. The first son was killed in the Iraq- Iran war in the mid-eighties. They lost their second son in an ordered assassination operation launched by the regime of Saddam Hussein at the beginning of the nineties. All of this made his parents fearful for him because they didn't want to lose another child; especially since he was the youngest son. The youngest sibling of the family was his sister, Ibtihal, his parent's only daughter.

Salah didn't consider himself an active member of his family, never feeling that he belonged in a way that pleased them. To them, he was the continual rebellious son, objecting constantly about anything they said and did, He was constantly upset; they were always comparing him with his brothers, who were considered heroes by the family.

Appearing out of the exhaled cigarette smoke was the face of his oldest brother, Ali. With his surly face and frowning forehead, he continually showed signs of anger and anxiety. These never left Ali's face. In his eyes, there was always that look of blame and accusation towards him. Oh, how much he hated that look on his brother's face and wanted to wipe it away. He wanted to remove it forever because it made him feel that he is a bad person, unworthy of his family's name and history. Ali always blamed the father for being easy and tolerant towards Salah. If it was up to him, he would have been very firm and intolerant with Salah's freedom and life that he was enjoying. Ali shared the power with the father. His opinion was always considered and adopted when it came to making an important decision for the family business.

In fact, Ali arranged the marriage of their young sister Ibtihal to Sheik Abbas.

Sheik Abbas was one of the Islamic militia leaders, belonging to a well-known family with great religious and political history. His father was one of the powerful religious leaders, followed by millions of imitators. They tried to follow his teachings, doing whatever he told them without question and imitating his life and lifestyle.

Ibtihal was unwilling to marry the Sheik because she didn't feel any kind of love towards him. She spent all her life dreaming of falling in love with a man who would become her husband, living the romantic dream of all young girls. She wanted to be a partner in a relationship. She wanted to practice free will with her partner, understanding acceptance and refusal. This was her life they were deciding about. She never imagined that one day; Sheik Abbas could be her husband. Even though she tried hard to resist her brother's will, she lost the battle and eventually married Sheik Abbas, as is customary in her part of the world and communities. Where she was born and raised, females had no right to choose. They didn't have free will in their lives. They did what the men told them to do: be subservient and appease men's desires. She had to accept that this was the way things were going to be for her.

Like all men in his country, Ali commanded all authority and power over a woman. He was uninterested in his sister's wishes and dreams. He believed that power was meant to be for men and God had created life so that men can be the commander over others. Since he was the oldest brother in the family, he felt he should get all the power and wealth available to him. Other family members must obey him and work for the benefit of the family. He also felt that, even if they have to make sacrifices in their lives, they must do it without question, especially women. This is what they were created for, to give themselves to the will of men.

This belief didn't sit well with Salah. He objected and refused to adhere to this way of thinking, sometimes loudly in Ali's face. Salah believed that before money and power, people need love, understanding, harmony, and romance. So he went against his brother's will and supported his sister's right for love and freedom of choice. But in the end, Ali pushed his plan, convincing their father and mother and eventually, Ibtihal married Sheik Abbas.

From that day on, Salah's relationship with his brother worsened. Ali began to hate him. No matter how much Salah tried, making every effort to fix his relationship with his brother, nothing changed. Salah's attempts to help in family issues were interpreted by Ali as rebellion against his authority. Nevertheless, Salah continued to love his brother and respect him, as he had done all his life. Salah never hated anybody. He knew that his rejection and revolt against people was not a personal thing, it was against everything he saw and didn't feel was right. But for him, all that the family did was wrong.

The Smoke Ghost

He exhaled more smoke, trying to bring out his ghost. He used to call him out when thoughts scrambled his head, making it difficult to make any decisions in his life. His vision became distorted as he began to see different pictures and shapes in front of him. Whenever this ghost came out from the smoke, he usually looked at him quietly, with a light, bright smile across his face. Salah used to wait for him eagerly; the ghost became very important in his life.

He respected and worshiped him, because the ghost would answer his questions, exposing the mysteries of life for him. He lit his way, helped him decide what is better for his life. This ghost was like a savior for Salah, a door he could open to get away from all his life troubles and misery.

When he appeared, he talked to him in these words: "Why? Why are you afraid? Why do you have doubts in your heart? It was you who decided to get a new life. After all that they did to you, all the pain and bad treatment you had to undergo. Now you doubt your decisions! Hold on to your heart. Have faith in yourself; there is a lot of power in you."

This is how the ghost talked to him. In a different way, his words had a special effect on him. He was totally not like the other ghosts that he used to hear about in old stories.

Salah sometimes felt that his ghost knows him better than he knows himself. Nevertheless, he had opposing feelings towards him. Sometimes he finds him compassionate. He is a good helper who is close to him and supportive of all his goals. He answers all questions that he has in his mind. Other times, he was annoying, evil and wicked, working against his will.

He couldn't believe that ghosts existed on this earth, but he had heard a lot of stories about people who had met them and confirmed their existence. As for him, everything started that day. The day when he challenged himself and decided to commit suicide, putting an end to all his suffering. He was totally handcuffed in his life. Unable to make choices according to his will, he has to submit to others in everything. Just like his name. He didn't choose it. His parents did, as they also decided to bring him to this life. Neither did he choose the type of life he now has, as others chose it for him. He was bound to them and their rules.

He couldn't continue to live in a community that wouldn't accept him for what he was. This was making him feel sick about everything around him. He didn't want this lie to continue any longer. This must end somehow and, he will put an end to it. He decided. To kill himself. This time though, things will be different. He will choose when, where and how he is going to die. He thought about this idea for a long time and found it the perfect plan for him.

He reached his hand under the pillow where his brother's gun was located. He had taken it days ago from his closet without telling him. He hid it under the pillow until he made his final decision. He held it in his hand, making sure it was loaded. He put the barrel of the gun in his mouth and took a deep breath. While he was thinking about what he was doing, his thumb was already on the trigger. It had been a long time since he used a gun, although his brother always encouraged him to use it. Time was passing. It was taking too long to pull the trigger. The muzzle annoyed him when it touched his tongue. He didn't like the acrid taste of the cold metal and felt uncomfortable when he inhaled the oily odor coming from the gun. Apparently, Ali had oiled his weapon recently.

All this made Salah disgusted as he frowned, what a way to die. So he put the gun back in its place and started thinking of another way to kill himself. As usual, when he was confused and needed to think in clearly, he took a cigarette from his pocket and started smoking it slowly. While he was looking at the white smoke that was filling the space in front of him, he thought it over.

An idea flashed in his mind. Kill himself by smoking. A lot of smoking will definitely kill him. This will be a new way and he bet that nobody had thought about this before. He will be the first one to commit suicide by smoking. It will be an interesting way to die. He will die slowly, relaxing on his bed and smoking as much as he can.

He rushed out to the store nearby, to buy what he wants. He was sure that the lady who owns the store would be surprised. This woman was a disgrace to humanity. Her store was the dirtiest place he had ever seen. The shelves were covered with dust and the walls drowned in darkness. No doubt it was a dark place. He never liked her. She used to yell at him whenever he went to get their national food assistance. Many times he argued with her because she used to steal from their shares. Not only him but, from others. She even stole from widows and orphans.

The strange thing about her is that, she prays five times a day, using God's name a lot while she talks. She quotes from the holy religious leader's words. She was a big liar and hypocrite. Seeing her ugly pale face will make him more certain of his decision, He will be eager to die and leave this world, because, its unworthy to live in this world if he has to share it with this wicked lady. He bought all that he needed from her with a mean smile on his face, leaving her in great confusion.

He went back home triumphant and confident about his idea. He entered his room and locked the door. He then closed the windows, making sure that all the openings were sealed by cramming them with wet clothing, ensuring that no clean air is able to get into the room. He looked at everything and saw that it was good, then stretched on his bed, and lit up his first cigarette.

By the time the smoke started to fill all parts of the room, he felt as if he was at an altar, with the smoke scent surrounding him from everywhere. The room became like a temple, full of incense and he was the worshiper, fascinated with its power. Gradually he became attached to it, unable to move or break its spell. He continued smoking, unaware of the time or how many cigarettes he had smoked. Time became worthless for him after this bold decision.

The color of the room became snow-white, indicating that the place run out of oxygen. It wasn't a big matter for him. He doesn't need it anymore, as long as he was going to die. Dying slowly without any pain gave him a feeling of happiness, despite the sense of heaviness in his head. Therefore, he stretched his body out on the bed, preparing for what was next. He had smoked a lot of cigarettes, so many that he couldn't count.

After many hours, he fell into a coma, paralyzed from head to toe. Only his hand was moving, raising the cigarettes to his mouth. Many shapes and pictures started to appear before him, running in front of his mind's eye. There were pictures of different people whom he had seen before, many years ago. They started appearing consecutively, one after another. The movie of his miserable life and events was moving in front of his eyes, from his early childhood to the struggling events with family. The neighbors, his early school friends and teachers, the mosque and its Imam, all kept rolling over and over. Then, everything stopped. He lost touch with everything around him. Only the white color was everywhere.

Suddenly, a shadow, a human shape jumped out at him. At first he thought it was a product of his imagination, due to long hours of smoking countless cigarettes. But, a sound came out from the shadow, speaking in a clear and strong voice:

"Hello Salah."

He turned around, looking for the source of the sound. It was just a pale shadow.

The voice repeated, "Hello Salah."

He stared at the shadow, wondering, what is this. Is it someone hiding? Or, is it just the hallucinations that come before death. How could this be true? It is impossible for any human to be with him in this room. He had locked it very well. This must be a death hallucination.

The voice came back again, this time asking him,

"Why you are trying to commit suicide?"

Salah thought again. This voice sounds so real! But, who is this person? Maybe it is one of his family talking to him. Or a friend he used to now. But how could he manage to enter his room? He was sure that the door was locked. Addressing a question to the shadow, Salah replied:

"Who are you? How did you get in here?"

The voice answered, "Me!!... You know me. I am the one you called for, so here I am now."

"But, I don't know you so, how could I have called you?"

The voice said: "you did. All the smoke and the cigarettes are signals that you want me here. You asked for me to appear and exist in your life. I answered your request. So here I am."

Salah now realized that the voice was coming from a true source. "I don't know who you are!" he replied uninterested: "I am not sure what you are saying is true. You have come at the wrong time because nothing is important for me, not even you"

But the voice kept repeating, "Why you are trying to commit suicide?"

The shadow was persistent, so he had to answer his question: " I... I... don't know. This was the best way I could find to express myself. Maybe I feel depressed with my life. Or, it was just an escape from facing the reality that, I can't handle it anymore. It's all mixed up in my head now; it's making me unable to recognize my inner intentions" he then asked: "But you didn't tell me who you are and how you got in here?"

"Me? I told you before who I am! I am your ghost. I came to you because you called for me."

"What? I didn't call you?"

"Yes, you did. You smoked all these cigarettes. All the smoke was enough to seek me out and bring me to you. It's has never happened that a man has smoked this amount and is still alive. The point you have now reached made it possible to connect with ghosts. So, I came to you"

"I did this!? That's incredible! I mean, that's amazing!"

"Yes, you did this. And I am here now to be with you, to guide and counsel for what's best of your life. A person like you must have a ghost like me. And always remember me dear Salah. Inside of you there is a lot of power and gifts. You need to show it all to the world. Today, you have certainly proved that you have a strong will to do that. Otherwise, how could you take on such a decision as to commit suicide unless you are a strong person?"

Salah gradually regained consciousness, trying to make sense of every word he had heard in his mind.

The smoke taking the shape of a person said: "Believe in yourself. You have more than you think and more than other people think. Don't let this world defeat you. Don't give up quickly. Not everybody could've smoked all of these cigarettes and remained alive."

As Salah was listening to him, a wave of comfort immersed his soul and felt his life worth something now. Although he did not understand the meaning behind this talk, he needs to do exactly what this ghost is telling him. Hold on to his life, be strong, and show his family and the other people around him that he can achieve a lot of things.

The ghost continued speaking: "Today I give you a new life. Today you are new person. You are different than before. Salah, remember this day always. This is the day you summoned your ghost." The voice stopped and the shadow disappeared as there was loud knocking at the door and loud voices: "Salah, my son, open the door... Salah... Answer us please! What is going on? Are you still alive? Open the door!"

14

His father and brother were trying to break the door down and get in. Smoke had filled not only his room but the entire house. Finally, after many attempts, they broke into the room. But the moment that they were inside, they were astonished with what they saw. Salah was sitting on the bed with a little smile on his face. His skin color had turned to white and there was still a cigarette in his hand.

The Truth Comes from a
Bloody Scene

Salah's problem was his rejection to the environment in which he was born and raised. When he usually looked to his family and his own people, he got this feeling, strange and inapprehensible. Not that he was uncomfortable with them, but he was missing out on something that was going on around him. He didn't know exactly what it was, so he kept looking for the unknown, the missing thing. He used to try anything new and strange in his life, whenever he had the chance. Those things he saw in front of him or heard about from others. He was always looking for a chance to get away from his reality. Perhaps, by doing so, he will find new people, different from his own and join them in their beautiful world. That world would be more tolerant and spectacular, full of love, free of hatred and distrust; a world in which he could embrace his existence and be happy, never being dominated by others. An optimal world, he was sure that such a place must exist somewhere. He had confidence in finding a good life waiting for him. A life better than the one he has now, with people who are better than those around him.

He was assured of this difference and lack of harmony within his community the day he watched the news on television. It was afternoon and he couldn't take a nap because of all the shouting and yelling from the kids who used to play in the street near the house. The news showed a film about a leader of some of the armed Islamic organizations. The man was cloaked in a black hood, which allowed only his eyes to be seen. He started by quoting verses from the Quran, reading a statement from a piece of paper in his hand. All the while, he was holding a machinegun in his other hand. He was threatening God's revenge, which is coming to strike the infidels of this world. He mentioned many western countries that are going to burn in hell.

Behind him, a black flag hung, written on it "La Illaha ila Allah, Muhammad Rasool Allah". In front of him, an American hostage was on the ground with hands tied to his back. The kneeling man was very calm, submissive to his kidnapper. Like a peaceful sheep, he was accepting his destiny. The masked man spoke a lot of Arabic in a loud voice, waving his hand. Then, after finishing his speech, he took a wide bladed knife and started slaughtering the American hostage. It was odd how the masked man took his time in what he was doing; moving the knife up and down slowly with his foot was on the hostage's chest. The hostage was whining with faint sounds, completely

17

powerless. The blood covered the man and poured out everywhere. After he finished, the strong, bloodied masked man acclaimed three times:" Allah Akbar". Salah was frozen in his place and felt dryness in his throat. His eyes bulged like billiard balls that were going to jump out of his face.

He had never seen something like this before on TV and started asking himself: can this be true? Is it real? A man can kill others this way? How can a human being become bloodthirsty to this extent? Killing people and using God's name to justify this? Could this be God's way? Is this his goal and purpose for humanity? Does God encourage people to kill each other? Giving permission to his followers to accomplish his will and purify the world, making it better this way. Can God expect people to love him if he treats them like this? Making them behave like animals, worse than beasts. A lot of questions stormed through his head about this God that his family and religious mentors used to teach him about.

For some time, he stood motionless, devoid of thought. Then, many pictures from his memory passed before him. He remembered when he was a child, playing with other kids as he was going to school in the early morning, afraid because of stray dogs and animals. He remembered the people packed into the weddings: the air filled with the smell of gunpowder from gunfire: the funeral of his grandfather. He remembered him with his long amber rosary in his hand. He used it to pray, repeating the name of God with each bead he dropped. One time, he asked his grandfather about God:

"Grandpa, is it true that God doesn't love me anymore?"

"No, this is not true my dear. Why would you say something like this?"

"Mama told me that if a boy is not well behaved, and continues to tell lies, God won't love him anymore and will throw him into hell. That's what she said. She was very serious when she said it; I don't want to be burned in hell."

"Well, did you lie?"

"Yes, I did."

"Ok honey, lying is a bad thing but, God doesn't throw anybody into hell. He doesn't treat us in such a way."

"I don't understand. How can this be grandpa?"

"God loves us and wants us to love him too. We shouldn't be afraid of him. He will never send you to hell. He doesn't spend his time throwing people into the fire."

The image came back to him; a picture of his grandpa, sitting on his old mat. Above his head on the wall hung his sword, with its crafted grip and inlaid with shiny colored stones. This sword was unique. The blade was one of the strongest and sharpest in the entire world. His grandpa said it was made from a special metal, taken from a meteor that fell in the desert near to the old city of Najaf in the south of Iraq. His ancestors used to live there.

The sword became an emblem for Salah and his family. Oh, how much he loved this sword and loved his grandpa. He loved grandpa so much that he wishes he could talk with him now. He still remembers his smell; how it is still stuck in his nose. Grandpa had a strong smell of tobacco emanating from his clothes as he used to spend many hours a day rolling cigarettes. Watching him was Salah's favorite thing to do, observing his hands rolling the small flimsy white papers with a smile on his face. He was wrapping the cigarette paper as if his life had passed away. Quietly folding his long years, the bad ones and the good, he finally lights a fire, as if to burn it all away then, exhales the smoke.

His grandpa used to call him and say, "Come on Salah. Tell me. Who do you love more; me or your grandma?" He used to play and make jokes with him, both laughing together. But, he knew that he loved his grandpa more than everyone. He always felt secure and safe with him. Till now, he remembers his face, engraved in his memory. A face of peace, full of wrinkles, the hard long years was marking their way on that face. The black headband on his head he never took off, only when he went to sleep. Sometimes in the middle of the day, when his grandpa was usually enjoying his nap, it was a golden opportunity to sneak in to the room and take that headband. He was obsessed with its circles twisted shape, the strings and the spherical ends. He really wanted to play with it. He used to hold it in his hand and put a big pillow underneath him, acting like a cowboy riding a horse. He would hold the headband in his hand, like a whip, gathering the cattle and imitating the western American movies he used to watch on TV. He would whip the air and shout, "Come on, come on". One day, while he was playing like this, yelling loudly, he fell on the ground and made a big noise, causing his grandpa to awake. So, he ran away and hid under the couch, afraid of the consequences for breaking the rules. He knew that he shouldn't have played with his grandpa's headband and interrupted his sleep. Then grandpa looked around the room, seeing his headband thrown to the ground. He knew that Salah was hiding somewhere. He called appealingly to him: "Come Salah. Come honey. Don't be afraid. Come to grandpa."

Salah replied: "grandpa, I am sorry. This is the last time I will do something like this. I promise I won't touch your headband again. Please, don't hit me."

"It's ok, Salah. You shouldn't be afraid. I will never harm you. The headband is not as important as you. You are more valuable than anything else. Come to me."

He walked to his grandpa and sat in his lap. Feeling safe and loved, he asked him: "you won't punish me because I played with your things and disturbed you?"

"No, I will not. It's just a headband."

"Grandpa, why is this headband so important?"

"Well, it's a symbol that pertains to our honor. You can't throw it on the ground; you will break the honor if you do so."

"If I break your honor again, will you be angry with me?"

"No, I won't do anything to you."

"But, you should. It's your honor."

"Salah, my dear; the real honor in our life is to love and take care of a young boy like you. This is the real honor! Go on now and continue playing. Enjoy your time. When you are happy, I am happy too."

At that time, he was too young to understand the words of this old man, who gave up all his pride and the legacy he inherited from his big family. He did so just to please his young grandson, loving him in such a way, pure, honest, and strong. This old man treated him in such a different way.

This kind of love and wisdom was unique in Salah's community. His grandpa was outside of his religion and its borders, different not only from all the family members but also from all the people he knew. It was as if he was from another planet and he admired this old man a lot.

Practicing love starts in early childhood. It is a very important phase for any nation if they want to improve and make progress in their future and build a clean environment. An environment where people can love, be honest, help and accept each other. If they just did as his grandpa used to do, playing with a child, they will learn a lot of good things. As of that day and, after watching the news, he became certain that he hated this God who orders his followers to kill people and slaughter them.

To Live as you Like

A man can be considered crazy if he just tried to correct some mistakes in his life. Salah discovered this when he attended the wedding of his Christian neighbor Carlos, a few weeks after his suicide attempt. He was encouraged by his father and mother to attend the wedding, for entertainment purposes, to get to know new people. Maybe he would be able to start relationships with new friends. They, his parents, did so because they were worried about his mental condition. The main intent was to protect him from committing another suicide attempt and provide a healthy new atmosphere for him, full of enjoyment and fun. Maybe this would help him to get over his difficult condition.

As soon as he entered the celebration hall, he was shocked by how amazing this place was. Lights shone from the ceiling and the walls in different types and colors. Flowers were everywhere. The place was crowded with elegantly dressed men and women. This party was on a very high level that he had never seen in all of his life. In his neighborhood, he only witnessed weddings that are held outdoors, where people usually block the streets and sidewalks, using it for celebration. Only men attended, as it is prohibited for women to join men at weddings and public events. These were the rules of the community and again, nobody can question it. Men sit on the ground; eat with their hands, all together from one big plate. The people in his area don't use spoons. Watching them using their bare hands, flipping the food and squeezing it between their fingers and then pushing it into their mouth disgusted him. Every time he asked for a spoon, they all gazed at him as if he was an alien came from another planet. Usually there is a lot of gunfire and of course, a fight between the young men at the end of the party. Eventually, everyone would leave for their homes; unhappy, gossiping about all the details of the celebration. This was his previous experience with weddings.

But this wedding was different. He had to wear a formal suit. He tried so hard to convince Shakir, his neighbor who had married over a week ago, to lend him his new suit. Salah was Shakir's identical size. The suit fit him perfectly, which made him feel happy and full of confidence, when he looked at himself in the mirror. He didn't forget to take Shakir's shoes as well. They were formal, black shiny shoes, but tight on his feet. However, he took them as he had no other choice. He was unaware of how big his dilemma was until he entered the party hall and the shoes started bothering him. They began pressing on his toes, threatening all of the self-confidence he had tried hard to build up on his way to the wedding.

He tried hard to forget it. He didn't want to waste his time thinking about his toe pain, unwilling to miss any of the details of this party. He was fascinated with the new things that he is observing now.

Everyone was wearing beautiful and shiny clothes, especially the women. He had never seen women look so beautiful and sexy in this way. Half of their bodies were naked; the dresses, designed in a special way that presented the beauty of their femininity, He could not take his eye off of them. He imagined that his mother and other old women of his neighborhood were with him at this party. When he looked at these women, he started laughing because they would call them whores. According to their tradition, a woman should not expose any part of her body to strangers.

He still remembers when his brother Ali rebuked his wife. She sat in the living room wearing only her sleepwear with no head covering. As he was sitting there watching TV, it was forbidden for her to show her hair to him, although he was her husband's brother. That's how Ali saw life, through the narrow window of the religious vision, feeding his obsession for power and control. He believed in everything the mullahs used to tell him in the mosques, never questioning the right and wrong in their teachings. The Islamic doctrines were indubitable for him. Sometimes, Ali looked like a monkey standing in the middle of a cage with a ladder, staring with sacredness at a hanging, bright banana. Afraid to climb the ladder and grab it by the hand, he was unwilling to discover the truth of the holy banana. The fact that it is just a fruit; he can hold it and eat it. That's what the naturalists did to him when they trained the monkeys who preceded him in that cage. Every time one of the previous monkeys stretched a hand to the ladder, they would open a strong stream of water at him from a fire hose. They kept repeating this every time he got up until he was faint and finally, gave up trying. He learned to stay still and not to touch the banana. The other new monkeys started to copy him unknowingly, even though they turned off the water. So Ali did exactly what he saw others doing who had preceded him. Standing there, day and night, overwhelmed with fear and ignorance, never laying a hand to the banana without knowing why. Salah considered himself totally opposite to that example. He wasn't a monkey. He will step up to that ladder, climb the rungs, reach the top and catch the truth. He stepped up with courage into this new world and took a seat between them.

After a few minutes there, he acquainted himself with the event around him. Relaxed in his chair, he began enjoying the party. He grabbed a cocktail and drank it all at once. He liked it so, he ordered another one. This was the first time in his life he had tasted alcohol. The drink was refreshing and delicious which made him wonder: why his family and the mullah's prohibit people from drinking? Even though they commit sins and do things worse than drinking, they only care about alcohol. Inciting people against it and forgetting other sins, they turn a

26

blind eye at woman oppression. Lying to each other, they have hatred in their hearts.

The pain in his toe started accelerating to an unbearable level. Oh, how much he hated that shoe! It is preventing him from his enjoyment in this new beautiful world. It was as if it was warning him not to go deeper, reminding him of whom he was; the fact that he cannot do what these people are doing.

As the music grew louder, everybody jumped from their chairs, ran to the stage and started dancing to the music the DJ was playing. They were all dancing with passion, as if they were in a contest, competing for something. They were interacting deeply with the songs and with each other. Men and women were dancing together, touching each other, at ease and laughing. They were enjoying what they were doing. He liked the scene. It reflected the type of life these people were living. Their life was easy, no complexity or taboos. A strong desire was pushing him to be closer to these people. He wanted to join them, get to know them better. But alas, how can he do so? That shoe is pressing hard on his toes, holding him back, keeping him in his seat and preventing him from movement. It was as if it was warning him not to go too far in his desires and thoughts, to be aware of the limits and remember who he was. He hated this shoe as much as he hated his life, which was too tight for him like this shoe. He hated all the people he used to see and meet. He was carrying a lot of bondage over the years, which erected high and thick walls in his life. It became difficult to break down these walls after they had become heavy and big, firmly implanted over the years. He is too weak to do this alone. He needs to be changed. He can't be like he was before. It's time now to change some of the rules in his life.

He lit a cigarette and started exhaling the smoke around him, calling on his ghost. A few seconds later, here he was, the so-called ghost appearing out of the white clouds, with a smile saying: "you can't resist it." "Inside you there is a big desire, you can't stop it. You need it."

"What? What do you mean?" Salah interrupted him "I need nothing."

The ghost smiled and gave him a mean look "are you sure?" Then he continued with confidence: "believe me, you need it and it's time now to step up for it."

Salah shook his head: "I don't need to prove anything to anybody. I have the power and the will to resist the silly things that don't fit with me" he said, reminding himself. "I am just a visitor here and after a few minutes, I will be gone."

"I don't think so" the confident ghost said. "You are dazzled at what you see now and you don't want to miss any of it. In fact, you are right to be so. It's such a beautiful place. The people are different and the women are attractive. Why are you resisting it? Your desires are normal. It's something natural in you. You want to drink, dance, smile and take with both hands everything comes in your way."

"Do you think so?" Salah asked with passion. "But, my toe is hurting me so badly." He looked down desperately at the shoe.

"It doesn't matter. Look to yourself. Your body is shaking; your legs are moving, affected by the music. Aren't you feeling happy because you are here?" Salah nodded his head, approvingly.

"You want to be one of them" the ghost said assertively. "Believe me, you can't resist it. And why do you call it silly things? Such things that make you happy, getting you to feel you are free again. They are not silly. It is needs; it is fact. Eventually you are a man who wants to live a happy life."

Trying to hold on the last strings of resistance, Salah said, "I have a good life. Everyone around me is saying that, my people...my family...they say that we have something good and better than others. We have rituals, ceremonial activities and commitment to our elders. We follow them in everything they say."

"That's right. You are a sheep." The ghost was mocking him. "You do what others tell you to do. You know where to forage and where the sheep go. That's what you are. That's how you have spent your life. You have spent it fooling yourself with all these lies, because people around you planted their rules in you when you were a kid. Look inside yourself at this moment, moving your eyes with gluttony over these prominent breasts, incapable of removing your eyes from them."

The ghost whispered in his ear with a gasping voice, "yeah...yeah. Beautiful are those white breasts, erupted are those naked boobs, just like a volcano, waiting for the moment to explode."

A beam of light shined in Salah's eyes as they were following the women breasts.

"Hungrily you follow the ivory, shiny thighs of the women, sneaking your eyes under the short dresses. Tempting and glorious these legs are."

Salah said, panting, "Yes, they are."

The ghost whispered in his ear, smiling victoriously and said, "their thighs are like chilly, icy columns on a hot day. You want to stick your mouth on them and irrigate your thirst forever. But like ice mountains in the sea, these soft thighs show a little of its beauty and slender The best part is hidden under the dress. You wish you could penetrate them and then, go deeper to enjoy unlimited pleasures."

Salah was sweating intensively, gasping for breath.

The ghost kept on pushing him. "Be aware of the beautiful hair flowing like a waterfall of fire. If it touches you, it will burn and turn you to ashes." The ghost paused for some time then said, "Yes, you want to be part of this world."

Salah calmly inhaled the smoke to remove it from his sight. That was all he needed; a few words from his ghost. He extinguished the cigarette and closed his eyes; he moved his hands down to his feet. Slowly, he loosened his shoelace in an involuntary movement. The ghost words worked on him. He took off the first shoe then, proceeded with the second one, He had fully surrendered to his desire, out of his consciousness and out of the boundaries of his world that had captured him for many years.

The sound of loud music, combined with voices of people shouting and singing was reverberating strongly in his ears, like falling water pounding in his head. He was completely unable to recognize and unable to figure out what it all meant. He was attracted to the crowd. Fastened to them as if a piece of metal that couldn't resist a magnet. He was lost in a big universe, with a need to be saved. He jumped up quickly from his place and, with one step, he joined the human flesh clashing on the stage, stuck to each other and sweating from head to the toe. He merged among them and vanished. Nobody noticed him barefooted; everyone was busy dancing and singing. This was the first time Salah let go of his fear and freed himself from his family's rules and boundaries. He did not care what people might say about him. He was crazy.

These were to be the last moments of his existence as Salah. From now on, he will be a different person, a new man who belongs to a new community.

The Wind Blows
Wherever it pleases

He got out of the taxi before arriving at his destination. He walked a few steps along the street and then stopped, giving himself more time to think before he entered the place. Although he had already thought about it many times, he spent the last few days imagining the place from the inside, trying to match it with what he had in his memory. The memory was simply feedback from watching the television and what he had heard from others. However, it was still hazy and an unclear picture to him. Christian life was a mysterious world for him and other boys in the neighborhood. There was a Christian neighbor living near their street, close to their house. He seldom had any contact with them. He only knew their son Carlos but, not very well. Carlos never played football with them, even though football was the game that obsessed all young boys. Carlos never played football and he was not involved in any kind of fighting, which happened regularly between the children. Salah's mother visited them a few times. She always talked about how great and nice they were. She thought well of Carlos' mother. On special occasions, they would exchange food with them. Like most Christians, they were good people. Nevertheless, he had heard different things from the old people in his community. They used to say, Christian are of false beliefs, due to a lot misbeliefs in their religion. They corrupted their holy book by misrepresenting the contents of the Bible. By faking a different one, they had strayed. How could people decide that others had strayed without knowing them personally? He couldn't judge them because he never was a Christian. He can only judge by what he knows and experiences.

So, with all the struggling inside of him, he was still excited about what he was going to do now. It was a very bold step to carry out, uncommon for a person like him to do. It was a great adventure. He very often yearned for adventures in his life, seeking not to be like others around him. He always saw himself different from his brothers and his neighbors of the same-age. He didn't know where he gained this behavior. Perhaps because of his grandpa's continual encouragement when he was a child. "Salah is a smart and clever boy, has a good heart and is different from other kids his age." His grandpa always said this when he talked to others about him.

Salah, as a Muslim, knows that if he was born and raised in his community, he has no other choice but to be a Muslim. He can't discuss it or question it. Nobody accepts any doubts in the religion. People around him believe that they are better than others, the best nation on this earth. So, must stay as he is--a Muslim. Any attempts to change this situation will be rejected. Should he decide to convert to another religion, everyone will abandon him. First, his family: Then, the community. They will be at odds with him and become his enemy. Finally, if he doesn't listen to them and return to his religion, they will kill him. Simply, it would be easy for them to do so. They will consider him an apostate and shed his blood. These were the rules of his religion and there was no way to change them.

Many times, he thought of his parents and how they would deal with it. What will their reaction be if they know that he has these thoughts? All these questions and objections to what they were all born into? If he exposed his refusal toward their beliefs, would they accept him as he is or are they going to follow the rules? Though he is their beloved son, religion is their existence. The way they were born and raised, it goes back many years with a strongly connection to their history. This has formed what they have now. They can't simply change the channel and be different. His father's law of life was, "you can't change everything in your life." He always used to say this. But, he is different. He will change his life forever.

He doesn't have to care that much about what other people would say and think. The world around him has changed and became totally different. People today can choose whatever they want and worship anything they like. It is freedom the world is enjoying now. So he should be able to enjoy his freedom yet, he must choose his own.

All of this was going on in his mind while he was approaching the place. From where he was standing, there was no way to step back. And according to what he did at the wedding, he can trust himself now more than ever before. He can do things he was unable to do before. This will be his second brave decision, to enter the church and attend the mass. This could be a new and exciting experience, regardless of what he will find inside. Maybe he will get answers for his multiple questions about God. He will get to know the reason of his existence and how to ordain a new path for his life. He could find the truth he was looking for.

Standing in the middle overloaded by thoughts, he lit a cigarette to kill some time. His ghost appeared and said: "you kept me away from you too long." The ghost smiling said, "I was certain you would call me soon. You are in a big mess. Don't worry though, I am here. I can understand all your thoughts."

Salah looked at the cloud of smoke, shrugged his shoulders and said, "You understand me! Maybe, but you don't know what I want."

The smoke ghost came near and whispered in his ear, "I know what you want. Actually, I know more about you than what you know about yourself." The cloud of smoke then started to increase, surrounding Salah, and the Ghost continued, "I am the only one who can show you the way to your real destiny."

"That's what you think! But, in fact, I can give up on you whenever I want, because I know my way."

The ghost giggled and said, "Let's clear what is going on here. You had troubles; therefore you called me, seeking my advice. And now you claim that you don't need me? How can this be? What a contradiction this is, Salah!? Until now, you are refusing to admit your weakness and fears. Don't try to lie to me. I know you very well. You are hesitant, afraid, and desperate for someone to help you. Yet, you don't accept the help. Anyway, it is useless for you to stand here. What are you waiting for? It's too late now to go back. Keep going and join the church. You have nothing to lose."

Salah nodded in confirmation and began to gather his courage.

The ghost added: "Your grandpa who loved you died long time ago, leaving you alone in this world. Love, of which you always dreamed about you couldn't have. Your family no longer understands what you want and you got tired of them. What else are you going to lose? Go ahead. Perhaps you will find what you are looking for here in this place. Who knows? Maybe there are answers awaiting you inside, answers for the clues in your life."

"I think you are right my dear ghost," Salah said approving.

"Of course I am right... you too! You are doing the right thing. How beautiful it is to step forward, to do something different you missed doing before. Fulfill your own will and not the will of your parents or brother. After what they did to you for many years, imposing their own rules upon you since you were a child. This has hurt you very bad. Now it's your chance to break down something that belongs to them. Those things they spent many years building. You can do it, break their walls."

Salah seemed to be content with these last words. The smoke ghost disappeared after few puffs, vanishing with the smoke.

Salah turned towards the street and continued on his way. Once he stepped into the outdoor gate and entered the church building, all eyes were staring at him. This made him feel disturbed and afraid. Gradually, his steps slowed, his feet became very heavy, hardly able to move them. But it was too late to retreat. He had already passed half of the pathway leading to the church hall. He had to complete his walk.

A different feeling overwhelmed him when he stepped inside the hall where the mass was being held. The place looked like a museum. Everything was clean and white. The walls were very high, with long windows, which allowed sunshine to fill the place. A pair of white marble columns surrounded the hall from both sides.

Silence prevailed over everything, except for the sound of music coming out from the big organ; heavenly, charming music was being played by a divine orchestra. Then, the choir started singing, as if they were welcoming him to this place, greeting him. While he was walking alone, across the path with quiet steps, he was taken aback by this divine scene. Again, he began to hesitate. Where to sit? Choosing a spot to sit down was not easy to do in this place because this was his first time being here. Choosing a place to sit could make his visit either a huge failure or a huge success. For a second, he thought about calling his ghost. He passed on the idea because it was impossible to smoke a cigarette here. Desperately looked to one side, he saw an empty space beside a girl who was praying.

He quietly sat down, trying to adjust in his seat, listening to the song which provoked him to motion. It was glamorous and great; he was taken with its affect, so he found himself crooning with the choir.

The words touched him deeply and tickled his lost soul. He was really living in darkness and desperately needed a light to shine and lighten his path. He wanted to hear God, to talk with him and get his guidance. God is the only one who can spare him from the desperate life he is living now, to give him comfort and peace for his troubled soul. He had became tired and consumed for the many years he spent looking for this. Finally, he found something, in this church hall. This holy place crafted and decorated with pictures, statues of saints and angels of God. This is surrounding him now, like a bird. He was flying in this heavenly music that flooded the place. This great song that is coming out from this angelic choir has marvelous words, deep and strong. The words express the relationship between man and God, clearly demonstrating how God's love should be towards people. The words were drafting a real partnership between God and man, in a different sense with real meaning. He never realized this kind of relationship nor knew God in that way. He had never felt like this before. God wasn't so close to him like he is now. Penetrating his soul, and redeeming his spirit again. Overwhelming him with unlimited peace, blessings flowed with an infinite love.

He lifted up his head to look at the ceiling in the hall. It was very high and bright, with side stained glass windows that were shiny and colored. The roof was supported by two rows of spectacular marble columns on both sides, which identified and lead to an elliptical alter. Positioned in the center was a stage with three steps, where the priest was standing with his white and golden striped robe. He was holding the ritual sacrifice of divinity between his hands. Salah noticed the man's face under the falling sunlight coming through the glass above the dome. His face reminded him of his grandpa. They both have the same grooves, the same smile and the same white, restful face.

When the priest lifted his hands up as he prayed, an image from his past flashed through his mind. The image was of his grandpa, as he entered the room and found him sitting on his old rug, lifting his hands up in the same way the priest was doing. He was praying to his God silently with a smile on his face. That day he interrupted him and asked:

"Grandpa, what are you doing?"

Grandpa broke his prayer, unbent as he sat, then replied, "I am praying, my dear."

"What do you mean you are praying? And to whom are you praying?"

"I am praying to God" he said, picking up his rosary between his hands "As human we need to communicate with him and we do so by praying."

"Who is this God?" Salah hastily asked.

"Well, that's not an easy question. God is the creator and he created us."

"Created us!" Salah wondered for a while. "Oh, I understand that. It's like when my mother and father created my sister Ibtihal, isn't it?"

"Hmm… It's something like that." The both went quiet while observing the falling beads through the rosary string.

Salah shifted his eyes to him and said, "Grandpa, I want to see God."

He looked at him and smiled "Dear Salah, God, is within you. You reflect the face of God."

Salah stepped forward and sat beside his grandpa, looking him in the face and said " hahaha, am I a mirror? "

As they laughed together, he stretched out his hand and took the rosary. He gazed at it and said, "I want to see what he looks like."

"My dear, he looks exactly as you do. By your acts, you will reflect his image."

"What do you mean?"

"I mean, if you are nice to other people, you will reflect his goodness. But if you are bad to them, you will not do so. You will show bad things about him."

Until now, these words are etched in his memory. It could be the reason why he had not accepted God, unlike his parents and other people used to do. No matter how much they tried in previous years, teaching him to do so, they were forcing him to adopt their beliefs and practice it through his daily life. That's why he went looking for another God, of whom his grandpa told him about. How much he wished his grandpa was here with him now in this place. He could tell him that he had finally found that God and this time, he will never let him go. He will stay close to him.

Face of God

One hour passed and he was still in his seat, contemplating and observing everything around him with a thirsty heart. He didn't know why he had that good feeling, with such a relief towards everything that happened in that hour. It was as if he was one of the church members or better. He admired Christian people so much, but in a different way. He liked their community, style of life, the relationships between them and their customs. But their religion! He didn't know anything about it.

How wonderful it was to know God in that way. As though he was looking at him face to face, he could feel God's love filling his heart, touching his soul, transforming him to another person. He feels like a real, free and perfect human. He was covered by this torrential love; it entered the heart and immediately turns death to life, dark to light, desperation to hope. How great it is to meet God and become a new person, a good person. Now he doesn't have to die to earn God's love, to gain a good life. He can get it all while he is still alive. He tried his best to convince his brother Ali and everyone around him that such love exists. They didn't listen to him. A great spiritual wave overcame him, as if his soul multiplied and became a million souls. He couldn't contain it all. These souls wanted to explode out of him, fly away through the place and reach everywhere. He was so happy that he had managed to come here, to challenge all his fears that had accumulated for many years, because of his old environment. He did it all alone, though it took him a lot of courage and strength to be here. He leaned his head down and started crying. His weeping brought attention from the girl sitting beside him. "Are you OK?" she asked.

He wiped his tears with both hands. He never carried a tissue or a handkerchief with him. He turned his head around; looking at the hall to find it was empty of people. He said to her," yes, yes, I am alright now. I just felt a little tired."

"Do you need any help? I can help you if you want." She put her palm on his shoulder and said, "We are one family here. We care about each other and love each other." She smiled and handed a handkerchief to him.

He repeated after her, "Love." It was a word he had missed for a long time, had almost forgotten it. He took the white handkerchief and looked at her face. She had a beautiful smile. He wiped his tears and then he passed the handkerchief over his face. It was soft, scanted with breathtaking smell, like the smell of her beautiful black hair.

He looked at her closely. She was a beautiful girl, with white skin, wearing a black short sleeve shirt which showed her white wrists, beautiful and solid like white marble columns in an old Greece temple. Her smile shines brightly, framed by her pink superfine lips. She asked him:

"You are not a Christian?"

He replied, "No, I am not."

"Are you a Muslim?"

He said, whispering: "yes… I am sorry I came here, but I don't mean any harm."

She replied with an assuring smile, "Don't be sorry. You came here because you were in need. I am sure you were looking for something. It's God's spirit who led you."

He hesitantly said "Can I ask you a question."

"Yes, you may."

"What is the name of this song?"

"This is not a song. It is a hymn and the name of this hymn is *To Be.*"

"What does it mean?"

"To be is the name of God in the Old Testament of the Bible."

"God has another name!" he replied surprised.

"The name they used to write in the Old Testament was *Yahweh*, which means, I am who I am; I am who is to be."

"Ah…I see. To be," he repeated.

"It is beautiful hymn, one of my favorites; we always sing it here. Did you like it?"

"Yes, it touched me so much with its meaningful words. But, there were parts I couldn't hear very clear."

She replied spontaneously: "I can sing it for you if you want."

He said: "Can you?"

She answered with enthusiasm, "Sure."

She started singing while he was trying to repeat the words after her:

> *I hear the sound calling me*
> *From the depths of the silent sea*
> *Here the light mightily shines*
> *Across the darkness, lights the shrines*
> *I see the sign on my way*
> *Slow down, listen, a voice can say*
> *Something inside me has a goal*
> *Shouting loudly over the wall*
> *Is it a man or Godly Flame?*
> *Me or him? Both the same*
> *I chose the task, far and alone*
> *For the rising rebel, I am the stone*
> *Up the mountain, you stretch a hand*
> *Pain and sorrow, can you stand?*
> *If I die, I don't care*
> *On the cross, I want to be there*
> *I chose to die not to flee*
> *It's what I am. I chose to be*

The sight of her singing to him was spectacular. The words were flowing from her mouth smoothly with fact. Her body was swaying with the music, as if she was dancing. He was fascinated by her passion, unable to turn his sight from her face or even blink an eye. The warmth released from her body dissolved all the ice that had covered his heart for a long time. It set him free, as a bird flying in the skies, moving around her bright face like the sun.

He let out a long sigh after she finished singing, and said: "How beautiful these words are, powerful and expressive. They invite man to look genuinely for God, seeking to unite with him."

She looked at him, with a lot of questions in her eyes, "You talk nice. It looks like you have spent a bit of time searching for something. You have to be very transparent and sensitive to feel these words and be moved by them."

He replied, unable to hide his weakness, "no, it is not that. I am too weak and poor to have all of what you talked about. But, I believe that man must find who he is exactly, to know from where he came. Seek the truth that makes his life have worth. That's why I liked the words and interacted with the song."

She interrupted him. "Excuse me; it is not a song as I said before. It is an h-y-m-n." she confirmed.

"I am sorry… I am sorry, it is a hymn. Pardon me; it's my first time to be in a church, so everything is new to me, I would like to know about your world."

She replied spontaneously, "I would be glad to teach you more about it. I will try to answer all your questions."

Though he was taken by what happened in the church and by all the new things he had seen in this place, which was a lot for the first time, he couldn't prevent himself from feeling comfortable towards this girl, more than normal. It was more than just feeling comfortable with her. It was a desire to be with her for a longer period of time. He was a stranger in this place. He needed somebody to talk with him and help him. She was like a lifejacket in this deep mysterious sea.

He asked her, pointing with his finger towards the altar at the end of the hall, "What are these big panels with engraved words, on the sides where the priest was standing and performing the prayers?"

She looked at the wooden panels and said "Oh, the one on the right is what we call the *Lord's Prayer*. On the other side is the Hail Mary prayer, which starts with the line that says: *Hail Mary, full of grace."*

He interrupted her and said, "And the one in the middle with big golden letters", pointing to a big board between the other two paintings, crafted in a different word font.

She replied, "That one", paused for a while and said "We…we call it the *Nicene Creed*, which starts with the phrase that says, *we believe in one God."*

This one caught his attention more than the others. He liked it and started thinking about the words, *we believe*.

How wonderful would it be if all the people believed together and agreed on one fact; to understand and accept each other? *We believe*… these words can unite people instead of dividing them. How beautiful it would be if the entire world was together. The people were all working for one goal, rather than fighting and excluding each other for the sake of power and control of the world.

He looked at the letters again but couldn't read the rest of it. They had used an old, uncommon font to write them.

It was beautiful paint for him, as though he was driven by his desire to know more about the content of this board, he asked her again "What is the Nicene Creed? Can you explain the meaning of the words?"

She answered him hesitantly, "I don't know if I can explain it to you. It's a difficult subject to be interpreted, which I am not qualified to do. Someone with more knowledge in theology and religion must interpret it you."

He replied with a look of fear in his eyes, "But, I can't just ask any person."

"A person with professional knowledge, not a stranger" she said cautiously.

"No. I can't talk with anyone else." He looked her in the eye with expectancy, "I can only trust you now." Deep inside, he hoped that she would be convinced with his reasons and agree to be that person.

She gazed at him with compassion and said, "Perhaps I can help you. But I will need someone to be with me because I am incapable of answering all of your questions. You are new to this matter so I have to be careful, and faithful." She looked at him thoughtfully, trying to remember something then said, "Hmm…ok, I know the perfect person who will be suitable for this mission."

"Is it you?" His eyes shone with hope.

"No" she said. "But don't worry. He is a good friend and I trust him. He helped me in my life some time ago; he is a good priest with a great spirit. He has a lot of knowledge. Moreover, he will be willing to help you, if you want. I can set up an appointment with him."

Her words had a magical effect on him. He would agree to anything she suggested, so he said, "It's ok. I don't mind, I can give you my phone number so you can call me to set the date."

For a while she hesitated and thought; should she be rushing into a commitment with a strange man; a man she knew for only few minutes?

But, she was unable to resist the voice calling to her, pushing her to help him; it was the voice of God, telling her to do this, calling her for this mission, to help Salah in his search for his destiny. To her, he was a thirsty man, looking for water. He is a seeker who has come to find the truth and learn more. He is a person in need. Her faith urges her to help such people who come to her, so she replied with determination. "Ok give it to me."

A glimpse of light shone in his eyes "Write it down, this is my number" he said. "I never let this phone out of my pocket. My name is Salah. What is yours?" He was anxious to know her name.

She wrote his name and number on her cell phone. "Thank you" she replied with a light smile, "My name is Vivian."

He thought to himself, her name is full of life, with deep emotions. It's like music to his ears, which elevates him from his tragic reality. Indeed, that name fit perfectly with her. He said flattering: "It is a beautiful name. I will wait for your call"

She looked at him, nodded her head and said, "Sure, I will."

After saying goodbye, Salah walked out, full of joy. Finally, he had a new world for himself, instead of the one that he always struggled with. This world has a different God, the one he was looking for a long time ago. A God that looks like the same one his grandpa used to tell him about. And he found a person who is willing to accompany him in his task, ready to hold his hand and help him to reach where he wants to go. He was definitely blessed and happy that day.

Fall of Footsteps

The road was beautiful. On either side lay big, luxurious houses with greenish gardens. He was pacing his steps, throwing his feet and tapping on the ground. With a cigarette in his hand, he was followed by the smoke cloud and the ghost within, trying to catch up with him.

Besides running away from the ghost, he was very concerned about his date. He did his best neither to miss it nor to be delayed, as he always does with dates. Usually, he has trouble arriving on time for his appointments; so he was late. He was angry at himself for disappointing Vivian. She arranged for this meeting and confirmed the hour with him many times, asking him to be on time. He tried his best not to embarrass her in front of the priest, whom she highly respected and valued.

He feels relieved every time he thinks about her. He can't deny his intense desire to meet Vivian again. She was really the right person that could help him stepping up the search to find his inner self.

He quickened his pace more and more, taking advantage of the tidy sidewalk. How good and clean it was! He was not used to these kinds of roads. Where he lives, the streets are broken; sidewalks are very narrow, full of mud and always dirty.

He began moving faster to get rid of his follower, who was very persistent to stay close to him. Finally, the Ghost caught up to him and whispered, "Don't go. I am telling you, don't go."

Salah replied sharply, "Shut up, shut up!"

The ghost refused to shut up, saying: "What do you think you will find there? Believe me! There is not that much you can get from there. No more than what I can tell you. Do you really want to go there?"

"Yes, I want to go," keeping his eyes on the road "and this time, I am sure of what I am doing. So don't bother me."

"Ok... ok, can I ask you a question?"

"Go ahead."

"Do you know why you are going there? Do you really know what you want? Are things that messed up in your head again? Be careful! If things get ruined this time, we can't fix it."

"Don't play your games with me now. I don't want to hear you any more, especially today. So you had better shut up," accelerating his steps to get rid of his ghost.

Shortly, he reached the house and stood in front of the door. He hesitated for a while and then lifted his hand to knock. He froze in his spot. The cloud of smoke joined him and the words whispered in his ear again: "you still have time to go back...believe me, you are doing something wrong. You will regret it." Salah closed his eyes, trying to avoid to falling under his spell. But the ghost continued: "why aren't you content with the things you have already achieved? You must remember. Everything was just an adventure. You can't go any further because you won't be able to control what happens next. I am telling you the truth; I can't change what is going to happen."

Salah looked at him suspiciously with every word he spoke and said, "But you said you are my ghost and that you will help me."

"Well, I can help you when you are in the midst of a decision but, you are desperate to go in. I can't do anything after you have made your decision. Therefore, listen to me and go back."

He turned his eyes to the doorbell button and let out a long sigh. A nice picture was still tickling his imagination; the picture of him sitting with Vivian and the priest. He spent all night dreaming about this beautiful meeting. He can't go back now. Pushing that doorbell is not going to be easy. It's the biggest movement he will ever do. It looked so difficult to him. He can't be defeated by a door bell. He took his time to gather the courage, convincing himself it is just a button. His hopes and dreams are bigger than just a button.

The ghost repeated, like an echo in his ears: "you can't do it! Back out...back out!"

He tried hard to close his ears, not to listen to his ghost's calls. Incapable of understanding why he was doing this to him, he had helped and guided him in previous situations. He had stimulated all this power in him, encouraged him to do whatever he wanted and to step towards places he was afraid to reach before. Why he is rebuking him today? Why is he preventing him from doing something good? It is difficult, this time, to listen to his ghost. Not today; after he has found the person who answers his long questions and takes care of him. This ghost is mean; he doesn't want him to achieve good things in his life. However, it was his fault for releasing him and calling him to be present. When he smokes a cigarette from now on, he will think twice.

Sometimes Salah seems weak to his ghost because he needs him. His ability to know everything and being able to make a decision comes from this ghost. He has the definition for everything. He can solve all secrets with his super power, making everything easy for Salah. He calls him when he is in a trouble and when he needs advice. But this time, he will not do as he tells him. He will not listen to him because he wants to attend this meeting. He has a desire to do it and sometimes, desire overcomes any kind of logic and will, even if that will has a strong, effective voice like the ghost.

Standing there for long time, he closed his eyes. He tried his best to isolate his will from other external factors. He was focusing on his goal of gathering all his courage, all the power that he needs and put in his thumb and point it at the doorbell button. With all his determination, he pushed on it strongly.

"Ring, Ring." He took a deep breath after the bell rang, ending all the conflict and struggle inside him. That is it...can't go back now. He has only one direction to pursue, which is located inside. He turned around slowly, dropped the cigarette and stepped on it. He then blew in his ghost's face with a smile of victory and said, "BYE BYE!"

The door opened. Behind it, Vivian shone with her angel face. She welcomed him with a beautiful smile and said: "You are late. But don't worry, he is waiting for you. Come in, follow me."

He followed her into a long beautiful corridor, decorated with spectacular colored pictures. When he asked her about them, she said they are a certain kind of art that was used in Christianity a long time ago. Mainly, it was used to explain the life of Jesus Christ and tell about other saints in church history. They call it Christian Icons. Those icons carried deep meanings in their drawing. He liked it; they were so beautiful, full of color with a lot of symbols. He didn't understand the meaning of all the paintings. The one he liked most was a wooden, dark cross, fixed on the wall. Fixed to it is a statue of a man, stabbed, bleeding from his side and dreadfully tortured. The way he was laid on that cross, with his head bowed down says that he died quietly. This statue touched him more than any other thing. He wanted to ask Vivian about it, but she was moving quickly because they were late for the appointment.

Finally they were at the reception hall, which was a big rectangular room, furnished in a beautiful and fancy way.

The curtains matched with the big rugs covering the floor. Big sofas surrounded lined the place and on the opposite wall, there were pictures of religious leaders of the church. Each picture had a long title written along the bottom in a strange language. He couldn't understand the meanings but obviously, it was their names.

She interrupted his wonderings and said, "Please sit down."

"Thank you. It's a beautiful place". He tried to be courteous.

"Yes, it is" she nodded. "Father Joseph did his best to furnish it and he did a good job. It is here that he meets with people. He works in his office to manage to the church needs and he also sleeps in this building."

"And you?" he asked hastily.

"Me? What about me?" she replied surprised.

"Sorry. I mean do you live here?" He couldn't stop himself from asking this question.

"No. I live in an attached building."

He was relieved with her answer. "Do you think I am being nosy?"

"No, why do you say this?"

"Because I am asking you a lot of questions."

"That's normal. It's a new world for you. You have the right to ask and get answers."

The word "right" makes him feel that he is a real human being, wishing that he could get his ghost here to show him that he was wrong about his objections to this meeting.

She continued to tell him more details about this place and the priest he was going to meet. All the while, he was pretending to be listening. In fact, he was thinking more about her than understanding what she was talking about.

It's a real fact now; he is with a beautiful girl, alone for the first time in his life. He looked around; exploring the surrounding walls. Then, he fixed his sight on the closed door. He wasn't in need of any ghost telling him that he was not at the right place. A strange feeling gathered inside him, driven by the idea of being with a woman in closed room. According to his traditions, people believed that a man and woman are not to meet alone in a closed room, unless Satan was the third person with them, tempting them to commit a sin.

But why should there be bad spirits and devils when men and women come together? Why couldn't it be God who brings them together? God is everywhere. He can be here now, right here with them in this room. He is actually leaning more towards this idea, of God being between them. It made him feel more relieved and more secure. Feeling higher and superior rather than always mistrusting the control in the relationship. There must be good intentions in life. Trust between people makes it possible to create a mature human. There must be motivation to project good things in our life, instead of presenting meanness and mistrust to others. This was always reflected by the environment he was born and raised in and when he was a child. What is learned in childhood will remain for a long time, even after many years and when he becomes a man. He is still affected by these kinds of ideas, even though he tried his best to defeat and overcome his roots. It was not easy to do so, especially while she was talking.

A spirit that talks with and tempts people is exactly like the ghost he has. That's why people were afraid of ghosts and spirits. But who says that all ghosts are bad? The ghost he has is a different one; he is good and unique, one of a kind. Actually, he wished that he had met him a long time ago. Maybe if he had met him, his life wouldn't be a mess, like it is now. Yeah, sure. This ghost was a good companion at least. Without him, he wouldn't be sitting here with Vivian. The only exception was his madness and objections towards the ghost when he was trying to ring the doorbell. But, it was easy for him to handle it.

The cure for this ghost's disturbance was to turn off the cigarette. Exhale the smoke and that's it, the ghost is gone. He can be free to do whatever he wants.

She was still talking. It's like beautiful music when she talks. He had never heard such a soft voice in all of his life. It was as if he was flying like a bird while she was talking. Drowning in her black eyes, it was like falling into a deep well, unable to see the bottom or define its depth. He just kept falling, deeper and deeper, until he totally lost himself. He kept looking at her to satisfy his thirst; due to the harsh life he had spent in a dry, arid desert.

Again, she interrupted his fantasies and said, "is there something wrong?"

"No" he said, controlling himself. "Everything is ok."

"Are you afraid?" she asked.

He stammered and said, "I…I am confused. Everything is new to me. I am sorry."

"It's alright. Don't be afraid. I am here and won't leave you. I will try my best to help."

She gave him a friendly pat on his hand that made him go crazy this time. Her touch restored his soul. He is now sure that there is always a second chance; that life could give back more than it takes. How nice it is that God has chosen this girl to be the one to accompany him in this new life he is discovering. She helped him regain his hope; he is now ready to walk all the way to the end, as long as Vivian is with him.

She asked for his permission and left the room, leaving him alone to think. Another silly idea started forming in his head, which annoyed him a little bit. He tried hard to get it out of his head. Nevertheless, it came back to him with different memories from the previous years when he was a teenager, talking with other boys his age. They used to tell stories about girls. He heard them talking about how easy was to get Christian girls to become a girlfriend, because they have a different life from theirs. Christians, in their life, enjoy a lot of freedoms. Girls can do whatever they want, wear whatever they wish and go out with boys, without any boundaries or restrictions from their parents. He even heard that if you friend a Christian girl, she will give you whatever you want. She may go to bed with you, within a short period of time and you will enjoy sex for a long time with her. Yes, that was usually what young, miserable boys in his neighborhood used to say about

Christians. People, in general though, used to look to the Christian community as reachable people, without difficulties. He still remembers another point of view from the old people that Christians are good people and trustworthy. They always tell the truth and never lie or steal. His grandpa had a saying and used to repeat it: "Good for you if you have a Christian neighbor. You can sleep safely, assured that your family and properties are also safe."

Ten minutes had hardly passed. He spent it struggling with his thoughts. She came back, holding in her hands a tray with a nice cup of coffee. Immediately, her smile filled the room once she entered. He missed drinking coffee, because people only offered him tea. He was desperate for a change to drink something different than what he used to drink.

She served him gently and said, "Now I need to tell the priest that you are here. Excuse me again."

"Take your time," he said.

She came back a few minutes later. This time, she was accompanied by the priest. He stretched out his hand to greet Salah and introduced himself. Then they all sat down.

Father Joseph was an old man in his late sixties. He was wearing casual pants and a shirt. He was burly, with very sharp eyes, slow when he moves but, he looked approachable to others when he looked at them. He started by asking Salah some questions about him and his family.

Obviously, Vivian has told the priest everything about him and about his search for the truth. Father Joseph knew that he was at the church that day. After a long conversation, the priest said, "We are open to all other people, no matter what their religious background is. The church accepts everyone, I am sure you know this. You can also read it in the church history about how tolerant and accepting the church is for others. In fact, a lot of Muslims used to come frequently and visit the church. They adore Mother Mary and light candles in front of her statue. We've always had good relationships with Muslim leaders and mosques sheikhs. We go to them and they come to us." He paused then stated, "After all, we all worship the same God and we love people. This was the message of Jesus to the world; He came to declare love and forgiveness for all."

Life is Chopped Ends

Vivian was sitting between Salah and the priest. Looking at them while they were talking, old memories came back from her childhood. She saw herself at the beginning of her life, when she started looking for the truth, seeking something meaningful and asking lots of questions like most teenagers. As usual, God was the first thing she started with. She wanted to know him more and why he sent Jesus. She wanted to know what he wants us to do in our life and then, how to know our path and follow it.

She saw herself in Salah. With all of his questions and his boldness, he was able to come here to this strange place and meet new people. Though he didn't know them, he trusted them. He was definitely brave by challenging his family and his community with all their rules. She knew it was not an easy thing to do, especially for a person like him. She faced the same situation at the beginning of her search. Her parents were misunderstanding her and voicing their objections towards her decisions. But, she deeply wanted something different at that age when she drew a beautiful picture of her future. In her world, everything should be perfect. Love was one of the most important things she dreamed about and it should be the best thing to happen to a girl like her. She loved God so much; she could share his love and the love of a man. This was happening as she was growing into becoming a woman; that age when all of these feelings started developing inside her. Love has to be perfect; exactly as God's love. It must be holy, with no faults or flaws. Therefore, it has to be a perfect man to share this love with her; one that is strong and ideal, with principles. He must love God and live to be like him. Such a man will help her to accomplish her calling, to become holy and live in His divine presence. In her thinking, love must not be something that is ordinary or a causal relationship between two different people. It must be different and special, like the love she used to read about in stories of the Middle Ages and old myths. She dreamed of a person who would take her far away from all her weaknesses and family troubles she was suffering from. Understanding and absorbing her, with him, she will get away from everything bad that surrounds her.

This was her dream; however her reality was something else. This was not easy for her to accept. Her father was overloaded with many family duties and life's demands. He worked all day long then, spent nights drinking and smoking with his friends. Her mother was good at spending every penny of her father's money. This caused them to quarrel about family financial issues. Mother spent all her time visiting her relatives and other women in the neighborhood. She rarely had a conversation or talked with Vivian, who had grown up without much attention or interest from her parents.

Literally, she had grown up alone, without feeling any love or protection from her family. The only open door for her was the church at the end of their street. So, she directed all her questions and efforts there. That's what people usually do when they feel unhappy in their life. They start looking for an escape from the feeling of failure. They find no hope in anything around them, neither in their family, friends nor the community. In that moment, people turn to religion; drowning themselves in it and adapting all religious practices. That was exactly what Vivian did. She ran to the church. Clinging to it with all her might, she asked for hope and answers. Religion usually takes us in and promises us that everything will be fine and all solutions for people's problems will be solved. Gradually, people find that not all promises are fulfilled. In fact not one of them was close to fulfillment. The clerics then fail to explain why God doesn't answer their prayers. Why is He like this and why does religion look fake? They appear to be incapable of helping people. They even can't help themselves in this burning world. So, they try their best to manipulate and control people's lives. The clerics don't want to lose their power. By doing this, they direct all people to what benefits them most. They keep it all going because they have no other choice or they will lose their own followers. People fall in this trap; finding themselves in the middle of a maze, where they lose their direction in life and start to spinning around in circles. Many times Vivian questioned herself, does God loves me? She read in the Bible that Jesus came to us so we could have a better life. But in reality, she has had a worse life, even when she tried so hard. Her life didn't change. She grew sick of everything that she was taught and told. Everybody wanted her to be a good girl and listen to what the old people said. If she did so, God would love her and give her whatever she asks for. She did all of this for many years, with all her heart yet, her wishes didn't come true. Eventually, she hated being a good girl, just to please others without getting what she wanted. Why did people always set conditions in order to accept her? Why can't they just accept her for what she is without the need for her to change? Can't they just accept her weaknesses, desires, fantasies and thoughts?

She was unable to tell anyone what was inside her or how she was thinking. Once, when she shared her thoughts with others, it turned out very bad for her. She was eight years old and remembered this incident very well. It happened in religion class, when she asked her teacher, Mrs. Shadtha: "You said that God is here and he can hear us. Yesterday, I prayed and called out to him many times, but he didn't answer me. So, how can He exist if He doesn't respond? Can you answer me?"

Mrs. Shadtha was a middle-aged lady. The only thing she knew about religion was to obey the rules and apply discipline. She answered her in a rude voice, saying: "Vivian, you can't say something like that about God. You will be called an infidel by denying God's existence. It is the biggest sin in the world and you will be punished for that. Be careful. God doesn't love kids who ask a lot of questions." This answer was a shock to her and stayed in her memory for a long time. The word infidel had a worse impact on her at that age. She didn't know the exact meaning of it, but she felt it was a bad word. It is a word reserved for people who are not good and outcast from others. So, from that day on, she kept her thoughts to herself and never shared them with others publicly. Any questions that came to her mind, she would fabricate an answer, draw it within her imagination and then, store it in her memory.

That's how her day-to-day world was formed. Although it was far from being a reality and acceptable by others, it satisfied her enough. She started building a big net of dreams and hope. She refused to be formed by others and being forced to accept their rules. She was looking for a person who would listen to her and understand the troubles she had been through.

In that church, she met a priest and shared her thoughts with him, seeking his advice for her life. She wanted someone to trust him, a person who can keep her secrets and give her advice about her life's issues. And who is better than a priest? This man of God, who would sit with her and listen to her problems, he was seemingly different than the others. He can understand her and is compassionate. He never underestimates her issues, like her family did; to her he was a good listener, a perfect person at that period in time. After many meetings with him, she started feeling comfortable and content. Nevertheless, her active imagination was impacted with an overload of interest and compassion towards him and this caused her emotions to take a turn. Every time they met, she got this beautiful feeling of being with a passionate man that she missed a lot.

At the beginning, she didn't realize how dangerous the situation she was in could be; by being very close and under a strong spell of this religious man, whom she never doubted. How can she doubt a priest? She was only 18 years old, looking for a symbol, a committed spiritual man who keeps God's word. He has enough experience in life and with relationships. Unlike him, she was young enough to anticipate the risks, to prevent her from making an emotional mistake. Besides, she was too young and unable to realize the consequences.

From his position as a religious man, the priest used to meet people and listen to the details of their personal lives, their feelings and family secrets. But this time, things were different. This time, he interacted with her more than usual, sympathized and loved her without the regular boundaries; boundaries which had protected him all his life. He sometimes controlled when to engage or disengage with others. But this time, he wanted her, desired everything about her. He wanted to run towards her without any willpower to use his brakes. So he made jokes, exchanged nice gifts and text messages without being able to control himself. He simply couldn't resist his needs. This gradual feeling that attacked him, like a wolf attacking stray lamb crossed into his personal hunting zone. He was desperate for emotions, hungry for love and a female presence in his miserable and dried up life. His nights grew very dark. They were too long for a man to sleep alone in a bed. For many years, his emotional needs bit his body whenever he lay on his bed. This drove him crazy. Emotional hunger is worse than actual hunger. It is too hard to be prohibited from love and emotions for all that time; he was really at the edge of the cliff.

A Wolf in Lambs' Clothing

All the pain and negative effects from this relationship; she tried hard to forget. Yet, that day is stuck in her memory, not be vanquished. It was the day they had physical contact between them. She was sitting beside him, her patron, the priest. So close as to hear his heart beat. That day, she was full of desperation, talking about her spiritual stumbling and praying about her failure. Then, she started expressing her deep emotions and how much she missed being loved by someone. The big need she has for a man, to share these feelings with him. This lack of such feelings was influencing all of her life, even the spiritual side. It's causing her much pain in communicating and praying fluently with God. Then she started to cry, like any girl who feels weakness in her life. She cried to feel better, to get rid of all that load of inhibitions that had accumulated in her over the years.

She held back her tears for many years, teaching herself not to show her needs to others in her community. That's what a girl her age learned from the community, not to show everything she has, even if it is true. People will not accept her feelings and misunderstand her. Eventuality, they will accuse her of bad things. So to protect herself, she started putting layers in her emotions and life, until she became an unreal person. Therefore, her misery increased, as did her suffering. Her heart was fraught with love and passion, filled with great hopes for the future. Like a flower that opens at the beginning of spring, stretching its petals and spreading its scent around, Then suddenly, a heatwave strikes and brings her down.

Feelings of weakness and fatigue made her lay her head on his shoulder, seeking a moment of rest. The holy man responded, interpreting her impairment, as if she was calling him. He put his hand on her head, passed it over her hair, feeling its gentle smoothness. He was deprived of such softness. So he tilted his head slightly to her, breathing in the dangerous scent of her hair. This knocked him down. Her womanly smell while he held her was irresistible. Unaware of what he was doing, he kissed her cheek and clutched his arms around her.

It had the effect of magic on her also. Therefore, she laid her head on his chest and closed her eyes, unable to resist. She became deeply lost in dark tunnels of feelings and emotions she never had in her life. It took her far beyond her conscious limits. She breathed his smell deeply, as if as she was inhaling eternal life. Her heart beat accelerated, like a speeding train. Strongly it beat, pounding in her maiden chest. An emotional volcano eruption like this was enough to make her body shake. As he held her, it was enough to make each of them orgasm.

After that accident, she became more aware of how weak and fragile she could be. That holy man didn't care about the psychological harm he had caused her. That pain affected her life badly for a long time. It caused her internal devastation and she was unable to start again. Therefore, she kept to herself, staying true to herself and making a decision never to let any man manipulate her feelings again. She would focus on how to find her calling in life, to know God and serve him better. After all, her family fled the country, seeking asylum in the United States, like other Christian families did. She found her calling by working in the local church, helping children and teaching catechism at the church services. Gradually, she became more mature and aware of her situation and needs. There was no doubt that the price for learning her lesson was very high. Nevertheless, she was sure of God's love for her and his relationship with her had not ended. The connection between a person and God in Christianity is based on love; unconditional love. She depended on Jesus' words when he talked about himself. Her favorite text was from the book of John in the New Testament: "Greater love hath no one than this, than to lay down one's life for his friends." God is ready to give his son Jesus Christ for her to be saved. He is the greater love. He has the everlasting love, unlike others around her. He will not betray her, as they did. She trusted him forever and trusted what Jesus said in the Gospel. He will never lie or deny her, as he is honest and trustworthy. It's how he treated his disciples and the people who followed him. Never giving up on them or turning his back on his words and promises. How could he break a promise? That would be different from what he said about himself. He had sacrificed himself on the Cross to save all of humanity on this earth. So, she holds on to him tightly, taking him as that rock she could lean on in her time of difficulty. She held on to God, especially after the collapse of all the symbols and characters in her world, including her father, mother, religious men and all others.

Maybe this is one of the reasons why she was determined to help Salah. Even if this meant she would stay close to him for a long time. He reminded her of herself when she was lost, straying, alone and looking for any kind of help. She was very much in need of an honest priest to guide her in a good way. A priest to save her from her blunders instead of exploiting her weakness and needs; not to take advantage of her. Therefore, she took this mission upon herself; to accompany and help Salah in his search.

After the meeting with the priest, she endeavored to meet with him constantly, opening all available channels of communication. She would send messages, make phone calls and invite him to every religious lecture and meeting that she knew about. She was making sure he would stay close to any event that would help him know more and learn more. Salah replied positively to all her invitations. Being so close to her filled his heart with exhilaration. He was keen to not miss any chances to meet with Vivian. He wanted to be present wherever she was, no matter what the event was. He especially liked the religious lectures. He liked a lot of things they did together. For example, he loved sitting beside her in class and enjoying coffee and tea together at the cafeteria during the breaks between sessions. He memorized everything she said and wrote it all down. He even started to keep his dates and appointments, learning how to respect time. He started to learn more about the answers to all the questions he was looking for.

A new world was opening the door for him: a world with different principles, new traditions and a distinctive spirit. He made a new law of life for himself that says: "A man can change himself if he wants." He liked all of what he was doing. But, he realized that he would become closer with Vivian on a day-to-day basis, and that made him happy.

Enlightened Heart

With time, the relationship between Salah and Vivian evolved and became deeper. His feelings towards the world changed and became better than before. He was totally a different person. Practicing love means he was able to see the world in a different way. Now he can recognize the colors. Rather than seeing only gray, now he sees colors that make things more beautiful, meaningful and full of life, like a pink dream. Salah usually closes his eyes during such a colorful dream so he can enjoy it. He won't open his eyes, fearful of losing the dream. Fulfillment of his dreams was all that he was looking for. Now, this dream had become true. Eventually, he discovered another side of God, a better face, different than what he used to seeing before. How beautiful it is to see a big building from all its sides. You will get the full picture, and understand the design better.

One morning, he left his house and went to the street. It is the same street he used to cross every day, in order to reach the main intersection where he can get a taxi. He stood there and looked around with satisfaction. Then he inhaled deeply, as if he was breathing for the first time in his life.

Then he noticed the children, playing as usual. But this time, he saw them in a different way. They were like angels in his sight, peaceful and innocent creatures; despite all of the dirt that covered their faces and clothes. Previously, seeing them would trigger a desire to beat them all or lock them in cages like animals. He wanted to stop them from being annoying and making all that mess, like throwing rocks and breaking windows of the houses. They would play near his room, preventing him from sleeping and spoiling his noon time nap that he adored. He hated them so bad, because they had bad attitudes. They curse and say bad words loudly.

To him, they were just filthy animals, who would eventually end up joining different Islamic militias. They will join either a terrorist group or religious gang, which are both the same. But today, he saw them differently than before. They were just innocent creatures, kids who are lovely and pure, like birds.

He continued walking until he reached the sewer manhole, which was usually overflowing with stinky sewage. It made him feel very sick and disgusted every time he passed it. The smell was terrible; the place was full of insects and bugs. He used to pass by it every day, look down and spit on the ground. But, this time he looked to the sky, trying to breathe clean air instead of spitting on the ground. The sun was shining brightly, laying a touch of warmth on his face. He felt as if it was patting him on his cheeks.

After a few steps, he saw his neighbor, Sheik Jabber, also known as Abu Muhammad. He was standing in front of his house, but this time he didn't look away from him. He disliked Abu Muhammad, the old sheik who transformed his house as if it were a chicken hatchery. Instead of chickens he multiplied humans. All of his married sons were living in this house with their wives and kids. There were a lot of kids. Sometimes, Salah thought they had fifty children living in this small house. Whenever a son of Abu Muhammad married, they added an additional room to the house for him to live. It eventually became more than just a house; it was a compound. This was all that Abu Muhammad and his family used to do; taking care of their needs only. Disregarding the law and regulation, this family put a heavy load and a lot of pressure on the services and the infrastructure of the neighborhood, without paying any fees or expenses.

They didn't care about how much electricity they were wasting or clean water they were disposing of. Throwing garbage into the street, they never cleaned the front of their house. Salah considered Abu Muhammad the main reason for all of the lack of services they were suffering in this city.

He hated and despised them very much for their stupid desire to breed. Because of their stupid strategy on breeding, they thought that they will control other nations and eventually, control the whole world. Abu Muhammad wants to rule the world by his stupid ugly sons! He laughed at them and wanted to burn them; those animals, who don't understand anything in this life except sleeping with their wives and breeding. They were one of the black spots in his life. He wished he could wipe them from this world. Maybe if he did, he would save electricity and water and he would certainly rescue people from Abu Muhammad's evil eyes. He used to sit on the ground with crossed legs in front of his house, watching people passing by. He watched them, scanning them from head to toe. He never missed one. He would utter mean comments and criticize everyone, especially if she was a woman. He would say bad words at her and accuse her of various charges.

He had that look in his eyes, the look of self-satisfaction and feeling proud of his achievements. He seemed happy with this miserable world he had created around himself. He sure made Salah's life difficult with his stupidity and ignorance. He had turned the city into the worst city in the entire world. It was a city turned black. It fell into darkness and fears at night, because the power went off for many hours. The city became deeply silent during the nighttime hours. During the daytime, its streets were filled with terrible traffic, crazy demonstrations and bombings.

This made people not like the city nor could they stand one another. They wanted to burn everything around them. Thus, they keep opposing and rejecting each other, shooting and fighting for no reason. Salah hated Abu Muhammad so much so that, he preferred having a wolf than having him as a neighbor. At least when a wolf eats, it will be satisfied and stop. However, this man never gets satisfied and wants to swallow everything around him. But today, and only today, Salah smiled when he looked at him and greeted him. He couldn't believe that he did this! How did he do it? He couldn't tell! But he was sure that today, when he left home, life was different in his eyes….truly…man can change a lot of things in his life.

Phantom Truth

He headed for the street corner where Ghanim's tea kiosk was located. As was his habit, to have his cup of tea in the morning, it is the best tea he had ever known. The tea was infused with the flavors, dark and sweet. He sat down on the chair, sipping from his cup. He then sobbed, relieved as he smiled with satisfaction. He was happy with everything around him, this world in which he lived.

After hesitating for a long time, he took out a cigarette, gazing at it. He felt terrified at what usually comes from it. He was afraid of the smoke ghost, who appears and starts asking all those different questions, making him doubt all the good things he sees. The ghost was always trying to persuade him that all of the contentedness he is having now is only a phantom. It is only a reflection of dreams and good intentions that is running through his head, threatening his feelings of contentment and relief he is grasping for now.

This ghost knows how to spoil his good times, especially those times when he is taken with these pictures emanating from his imagination. At other times, he was useful, by giving him all the advice he needed. Usually, this ghost has every answer for all of his questions and knows about everything. He is able to explain the indiscernible facts to him. He can depend on this ghost's advice in order to make his decisions and to avoid falling into confusion and mental stress. Salah had this habit of imagining unreal things, which gives him nice feelings. So, instead of achieving good things in his life, he has to imagine it first then dream about it.

The dreams and visions he has are far from being achievable. His dreams were always a reflection of his conflict within himself and with others; he was aware of that. That's why he understood people in his world very well. Particularly, when people are deceived by a big lie and they start talking about this lie like it is real. Not only that but, they hold on it strongly, believing it to the extent that this lie becomes true in their heads. It becomes a daily fact. They start dealing with the lie, as if it is a real thing in their life; as if it has flesh and blood. They share and pass it on to others, recommending it as a remedy for all their troubles. The lie, after all was just a tiny thought in someone's head; that is totally anonymous to everyone. It starts getting bigger and bigger, until it takes over their lives and their communities. It will control them totally by freezing their brains and feelings, leaving them slaves to elusion. But, he bets that if they just pause for a while and have a chance to get alone with their ghost, they would admit that the truth they are following is just a lie. It is an illusion of their fantasy. This is what he and all the people were living with.

The Meaning of Existence

With the first whiff of smoke, the ghost appeared, declaring, "Don't be surprised. Everything is possible, since it's you who gives reality its shape, making it look as you want. It will take a form exactly what you want it to be. Do you believe that?! You... now like Abu Muhammad? Not only that, but you smiled and greeted him. Hey man, that is a big change," he said smiling. "You are certainly different, with more acceptances. Smiling and greeting this man that you hate more than anything else on this earth! As for me, I couldn't believe it."

Salah nodding seemed to be surprised too. "So am I! I can't believe I did it. This is weird; it is as if I am a new person in my thoughts, feelings, even my heart. It is like everything in me was replaced. I don't understand it all!"

The ghost said: "when you are changed inside, the way you used to see the world will change too. Everything around you will become totally altered when you become a different person. When you fall in love, then you will love all those around you, even your enemies. It's true and that is what has happened to you. Today was a clear example. When you comprehend God in a different way, your relationship with him becomes different. You begin to practice and feel new things. Therefore, you felt God's love for the first time in your life and you accepted your neighbor. God overwhelmed you from inside. He was not implanted in you suddenly. All this time, he was there inside of you. But, the way to look at him changed, in the same way of seeing other things around you. It all changed and became different.

When the ice mountain has drifted away from its position, everything will drift with it. This is usually what happens when we discover this inner spirit; the spirit we spend a lot of time looking for, even though it was there. It was always inside us, but we were unable to grasp it.

"How could it be inside of us all that time and we can't grasp or understand it?"

"We start searching from outside. We usually start with what is around us and try to find the answers from others."

"Yes, that's what we do," Salah affirmed. "When we want to know something, we start from others."

"To know something about yourself, you don't have to ask others," the ghost said.

"What should I do then?" Salah asked muddling.

"Well, first you need to ask yourself then, discover your inner needs. People spend their lives asking for it, but they never try to go deep, exploring their inner soul. This is where they will find the truth. There, they will find God and see him."

"Who can be guaranteed they will find God there?" Salah asked.

"The most powerful thing is a simple fact and, the simple fact is this: he is there always. You spend your life wondering: what does God wants from me and when should you start looking for your path. Then you ask where you should go to accomplish it. Isn't that what you were looking for?"

Salah nodded his head in agreement with what the ghost said. "Yes, you are partly right."

"I am totally right," the ghost cited. "You always asked God a lot of questions, as if he was going to send you a letter with all his answers. Meanwhile, you never asked yourself, because you didn't realize that the answer could be within you. Your behavior inconsistency comes with whatever answers and signs God sends you. You won't be satisfied with any of it and you won't accept it or accept your destiny; to walk in the path you were ordered to take."

"How could this be?" Salah said denying. "Can a person ignore real words from heaven; neglect God's answer that was sent to save him? I don't think so," as he relaxed in his chair. "I've spent all my life looking for something meaningful. It is impossible to turn my head when it comes!"

"Look to yourself and you will know that what I am talking about is true," the ghost grimaced at him.

"What about myself? Are you accusing me now? Since you entered into my life and I have been listening to you, I hear all your insane words; and your unbelievable talking.

If people know that I am talking with a ghost, they will say I am crazy."

"If you think talking with me is making you crazy, then why do you talk about my gaudiness? Why do you do what I tell you to do? Then sometimes, you beg for my advice."

"It is because I need you. That's the truth. I can't deny it now."

"If that is so, then listen to what I am telling you now."

The smoke stormed and spun around him. His hands started to shake. The tea cup that was sitting on the plate in his hand was clinking, as if there was an earthquake. But, he was the only one affected by it. The smoke cloud disconnected him from the world and the people sitting around him, and then the ghost said:

"The fact is, humans, and you of course, represent those who have ignored all of the answers around them. Do you know why?"

"I don't know" Salah replied, shrugging his shoulders.

"It is because you usually lean towards something particular inside you; a certain path or a specific answer. You search for it hard; wanting the events around you to be achieved according to your own wishes. So, you won't accept any other answers given to you, as long as it is different than what you want. You keep waiting for your specific result, pretending it didn't come. You go where your hunger and thirst leads you and that's usually to where your silly desires are. You are always far from being close to God or being close to the human nature you were created for. You want to pretend to be a supreme creature. In fact, you are the opposite."

Salah put the cup aside on the small table in front of him, then said: "This is not true either, because we keep praying and asking God. We are eager to keep our connection with him and with all our religious leaders who try to help us. I truly don't think they are doing this so, neither do I respect or encourage them."

"I will prove that to you. You always ask God to give you what you want, according your own desires right?"

"Sometimes, right," Salah replied.

"The intentions that you proclaim according to God's will are mostly not the same as the intentions you seek for your own benefits. When you pray, you say: God let it be your will. But did you or any other person know for sure if what happened was God's will? Did you check if what you are asking for is his will and not yours? It was always about you and what you want. Your wishes that make you draw all of these pictures in your imagination and then believe it all. You poor human…Despite all of your intelligence and a developed brain, you are still lost, in circles of illusions. You drew the illusions for yourself. I will say to you, Salah, the pretender, who represents mankind. I will show you where your intelligence brought you."

The smoke cloud inflated and expanded, forming a circle around him then said: "Your intent is to specify a personal thing in your mind and set it as a goal. Then, you pray for God to make it happen. It is as if you are asking for heavenly authorization for your deeds. You purify your scam and sins by using his name. You want to feel reassured that what you intend to do is surrounded by holiness, heavenly and protected. It is your intent to make everyone subordinate to your plans. By doing this, nobody can object to what you do. You pursue God to serve your purposes. This is how you used God, trying to connect him to all the details of your life. Yet, you don't obey his rules. Over the years, this attitude was improved upon and developed according to the time and place."

"You exploited everything you could, to get a grasp on what you wanted. Then, you formed it into your own rules and laws. Later on, these rules became more important than you; it possessed you and formed the life you have now. You transformed into a hollow echo, yet it became everything. Whereas, all you needed was a little confidence and true willingness. By doing so, you would have taken yourself out of the waste you suffer in now. This God deteriorated more than man; you made him a distorted source for everything in your life. You made him a source of sorrow and joy, pain and happiness, richness and poverty, sickness and health, peace and war, and many other things about you. So I ask you today, as you represent humanity, what do you want from God? And what does he represent to your humanity?"

Salah answered stammering, "People want to… communicate with him. They want to worship him; for he is the creator of the universe and also our creator."

"Ok, if he is so, why don't you do what he recommends? You've turned God into a flexible dress that must fit, no matter what your size is. To you, God is only the genie who comes out of the magic lamp and makes magic. Is this the God you are proud of worshipping?" The ghost said this with a mocking smile.

Salah asked: "If God doesn't answer and provide for our prayers, then what is he?"

"He is bigger than this. He is the feeling which beats inside your heart. He is the spirit that takes you far away from your reality when you close your eyes, seeking rest. With God, you are set free from the limits of your body. You are set free from its weakness and absolute materialism, which was planted in you and then, formed within you. With Him, you'll become a great soul which contains everything, small and large. In Him, you'll feel the world the ghost said, hovering around.

Salah was smiling as the ghost said, "God appears in your smile which you give to others. This smile has a magical effect; it gives them a feeling of rest, not just for a short time, but day and night and every day, all your life."

"This smile has the power to transform people; making them positive people and not just a mass of moving flesh. God is the heart that loves, without waiting for benefits. God doesn't wait for mutual love or conditional love."

"God loves the entire world. He is a non-stop giver. He doesn't consider loses or benefits. He doesn't sit there, doing the math of how much he did and didn't do. But, he continues to love unendingly. He is the love that creates new man. He transforms men, who were once a hollow person into a human."

"God is the comfort that you feel when you lay on your bed at night and close your eyes. He comforts you after a long; hard day that were full of troubles. Nonetheless, you find it beautiful, since everything that day was made for you by Him."

"You seek comfort, but you don't know how and where to find it. From the first day of your life, you start searching for it. However, until now, you have nothing. You are still fighting it, traveling and inventing for the sake of rest. I can give you what you want, I will give you rest. You can take it and it will be all yours. But, after a period of time, you'll feel bored. You will come back to me; complaining and saying there is no meaning in your life."

Salah gazed at him in astonishment, thinking about all of what he was saying. Then he said, "You have shocked me with your words! You turned everything upside down and changed all the things that have formed in my mind in the past. These things were deterministic, not only for me but for a lot of people. All of your talk is correct. This is exactly what we do. Tell me, how do you know all that?"

The smoke ghost answered, "I have been your companion and guardian all this time. Yet, you didn't know me nor could you even find me when I am here! You only saw me as smoke, coming from your cigarette. You didn't care to find out more about me, do you know why?"

Salah answered: "Why?"

"Simply put, you only think about yourself and care for your own needs. You see the world as a reflection of your selfishness. You didn't care to find who I am. I am the outcome of human beings thoughts throughout the ages;

that point where you discover everything about yourself. I am the fixed point which became the center of this spinning world, which is changing every day. Maybe you don't believe what I have said."

"It's not easy to believe."

The ghost said, "I expected this from you. Outwardly, I am just smoke, according to you, but..." The ghost paused as the smoke expanded even more, covering his whole body until he was lost inside it.

In The Beginning

The ghost spoke from inside the smoke cloud saying, "In the beginning, when the universe was created by the Big Bang, I was the smoke which resulted from that great explosion. I was the one who saw everything and followed everything that happened after the explosion. I observed the changes that were made to this world after it happened and for the millions of years since."

"Your age is a million years!" the ghost glanced with a sneering-like smile.

"Listen Salah, listen and learn. Don't laugh at me. You are just an infinitesimal part of this unlimited universe. I tell you the truth. No one knows about it, but me. I was there, watching and observing, keeping all the events and pictures in my memory. I am the material that saved all of the secrets the whole time. I have stayed as I am, preserving myself. My goal was to stay in this form, as smoke. Unlike me, you kept changing and developing over the years. Then, you became who you are now, a sophisticated creature, ready to erase all your past; losing the values that made you who you are. You forgot about when you were a primitive human being, hunting for animals to stay alive. I was there watching you. Sometimes, you watched with indifference at the smoke coming from the fires you made during the cold nights, without knowing what it was. Even before that, when you were only a small monkey, barely able to walk on your feet; you didn't recognize me. If you go further back in time, you used to fly through me. Yes; you were a fly in the beginning, flying inside the smoke, inside me. I bet you are surprised?"

"Yes I am, because I had never heard of this in history books or in any other books. It can't be true. This is ridiculous." Salah laughed at the ghost.

"You don't remember it because you kept changing. Every time you came to be a certain shape, you sought to replace it. This is how you formed the shape you have now. Your human body is the result of all the changing and replacing your different entities. Then, you became as you are now, a human.

I remained as I am; just smoke, floating around you and watching closely. I was dazzled at how changeable you were!! Moving from one shape to another, you were unsatisfied with any form you took. You kept changing all the time. You vigorously spent all your time looking for something new. This is the fact; you are what you are. It is your reality.

Even today, you are different from your grandpa, who also doesn't look like his grandpa. Both of them are different from their ancestors and so on. You are a human, preserved in a developing theory. Like a song, which fascinated you from the beginning, you couldn't stop singing it and following its trail for thousands of years."

Salah contradicted him: " You are accusing me now! Not all of your words are true. I didn't lend a hand in all that you have said nor have I denied my origins. It all came to me without striving for change. Like you said; I didn't exist at that time. Perhaps people who came before me, a long time ago did that but, I am just a result of them. You can't judge me for that. What else could I have done to fix something that happened many years ago? What could I do? "

The ghost interrupted: "No, you are involved in this in the same way. I tell you this and I am certain of it because everything has been saved in my memory, which is the source of all my power. I have unlimited power that comes from the huge data I have. I know everything about you and about this world. I still remember the luster in the eyes of Shoshan, the Sumerian keeper, when he saw a wheel for the first time. The wheel was invented in the old city of Ur in the south of Iraq, which is Mesopotamia. His eyes glittered keenly, wanting to own new tools in his life. He wanted to accelerate time and create his own destiny. The same luster was in Adam's eyes when Eve gave him the fruit of the knowledge of good and evil. They were both driven mad by it and couldn't resist breaking God's law to fulfill their desire. Adam's first step in his development was when he ate the fruit. The desire for the fruit was too much and he couldn't resist it. It was your ancestor's desire and they were ready to give anything they had for it.

Since that day, I knew this human was veering away from his spirit and good deeds. He will soon drift towards the shiny and beautiful things he might see along his way, unable to resist all kinds of pleasures. Clearly, this human was ready to sacrifice everything for the sake of more, using his hands to take what God was promising to give him. He didn't want to wait for God's rewards. He wanted to become a God.

It was your ancestors evolving nature, in that they were ready to give up everything they had for you and your own kind. The wheel was a great thing, which helped so much in your life. But, what you saw and then, the way you acted was the problem. It was the beginning of your soul's departure, which was lost. Until now, you don't know how to get it back. Without your soul, you are nothing; you are just flesh, moving around, breeding and transferring, influenced by time and space. You had no impact at all on what was going around you; the impact was on you only.

Your soul was the price you paid to gain all these tools and equipment, to build this world you are living in now. You filled your world with bad things. But now, you are trying to change it. That's why you keep calling me to come and be a part of your life,

Before me, you tried everything. You even invited in anything you could get to be a part of your life. You tried gods, angels and even the ghosts you didn't spare, though you achieved nothing. It is now time; time to throw away that wheel and get back to your soul."

The ghost formed a wheel of smoke around Salah that covered him from head to toe. The smoke isolated him, taking him out of his world, sending him deeper into history. Salah was listening, quietly taken aback by this scene. It was the most amazing thing he had ever seen. He sat still, closing his eyes, hovering in another world now; remembering the smiling face of his grandfather. How different he was from him. He had certainly missed a lot of beautiful things which were in him; the calmness, the joy, and his strength.

His grandpa didn't suffer from any diseases like he did, such as headaches and back pains. Salah spent his life afraid of people and his family, fearful of what the day might bring. His life was a continuous debate. It was as if he was a horse in a race, fighting in this world, which is full of beasts biting each other for the food.

He wished he could quietly sleep; sleep until he was fulfilled, like his grandpa. He wished he could enjoy his food. His grandpa used to eat his daily meal without being concerned about what he would eat tomorrow. He enjoyed eating the food slowly and restfully, without stomach pains. His grandpa loved all people and never experienced hate. He has never been jealous of anyone or afraid of what he was doing. He didn't have to hide his plans, because he never planned farther than the night. He was always doing what he loved to do, without being worried about it. He didn't have to praise anyone or to be a hypocrite in his relationship with others. He never sat or talked with people he disliked. In general, he was really a free man. Salah missed this freedom. He wished he could get it back.

That's why he is diligently seeking for new world in his life, to restrain his freedom. The pictures began to gather in his imagination and started organizing dramatically. The church, the sounds of singers with their holy music, this feeling of faith which began to grow inside him and this love he felt towards God, with the inspiration and constant moments he had with him. All these new feelings he experienced. He is making up for lost time and is restoring himself. He now can have a good life with Vivian; this beautiful dream and paradise, which he was looking for. She is like the seal which has been stamped on the official order coming from the heavens to set him free. Everything is now complete and clear for him. He has found what he was looking for and now it is impossible for him to lose this valuable treasure.

The smoke ghost interrupted him, "I see you have drifted far away in your thoughts." He glanced at him, "yes, she is beautiful and kind, but she is not the solution to your problems"

"What are you talking about?" Salah said as he shrugged his shoulders, pretending he didn't know what the ghost meant.

"I am talking about Vivian. She is a vital example to what I said about your abilities to turn against the truth; to seek your desires. Be careful. You may fall into a bad way with her, which would end your relationship."

Salah put out the cigarette quickly. He didn't want this dialogue to carry on any longer.

In spite of all his ghost's objections and suspicions with his intentions, Salah insisted that his relationship with her was for the sake of knowledge; nothing more than that.

This relationship, which had continued for a good period of time, had a negative influence on the other partner. Here's Vivian, gradually stumbling for the second time in her life and feeling lost on how to deal with men. Because of her need for love and passion, she has an active imagination, which usually led her to distant places. She would fall into unsuitable situations, influenced by her old feelings. It was unfair of all who were around her, especially the people in her life who were closest yet treated her unfairly. They played the main part in hurting her and causing her to be where she is now. She is alone, emotionally devastated, after she lost the most important and beautiful years of her life.

All the years she had to spend alone made her desires rise again, towards a beautiful love which she didn't get when she was a young girl. All these things finally came to her, deceiving her in the form of a relationship with Salah, who has his own share of issues. But eventually, she didn't care about these facts. She began to pretend there was an opposite of all this, ignoring the consequences of this relationship, She was unaware of her inability to deal with him, without being carried off by her passion for him. She holds on tightly to this relationship, which was feeding her desires and maintaining her hunger to love. This is especially important for a girl like Vivian, who was in her mid-thirties. At this age, girls are desperate to be loved by a man. Sometimes, she felt as if the train has left the station and she failed to be one of the lucky passengers on that train. She sat still, in a chair, waiting. Year after year passed, taking the brightness from her eyes, as well as all the opportunities. She lost her chances to love and be loved. She was left with only a bunch of people who see her as a person with no desires or goals. At this particular time, she was in need of feeling that she is still wanted and still attractive. She had to prove to herself that the long years of loneliness couldn't make her useless. Thus, hope can be restored in her and the past years are not a loss. There is always hope in this life. Likewise, opportunities are still available for her. The magical beauty in her eyes is still shining and active with life. She is capable of overcoming bad experiences like she had before and she can stop it from taking everything from her. There is still some hope in this life.

Trance

Here they are; unaware of how they reached this point. They were both naked. She was lying down beneath him and he was on top, panting and struggling to get his breath. He was like someone who had missed a train and is running as fast as he can to get on it; stretching his hand out as much as he could to catch the train's handrail and climb aboard. He was giving every ounce of energy from his muscles, which were shrinking and flattening, like a machine or a steam boiler.

On her back, she was completely submissive to him. Covered in sweat and groping parts of her naked body, she was making sure she was not dreaming. She was trying to catch every second of this event. She was holding herself hard so as not to faint, because of what she was doing.

She wanted these real moments to be proven in her life from long ago: to prove to herself that she was still alive. Whoever was around her now were unable to treat her unjustly like they did before. She now has her own free will, to do what she wants and not what others want her to do. She is fulfilling her emotional and sexual needs without their permission or blessings.

Each movement that Vivian did in this sexual experience made Salah feel good. With the moans and other sounds, it was all perfect. For a second, she wondered where these sexual capabilities suddenly came from. Considering that, this was her first time in a long time. Where did she gain all this sexual experience? She was moving and responding to him, almost like a professional, like a whore, with many years of experience in the business. It was weird to think about herself this way! With all that she had been through before, it made her realize that immorality of body is easier and less reprehensible than immorality of soul. All of what has been taught doesn't matter anymore. During these intimate moments, she was retrieving important feelings which were neglected throughout her life.

When Salah returned home that day, a tinge of sadness hit him. Once he entered the living room, he was met by his father, who was in an agitated state. He was trembling and shouting while watching the news. Apparently, there were battles going on in the country. Large armed groups, calling themselves the Army of the Islamic State in Iraq and Syria, dominated the city of Mosul and the Iraqi army had collapsed.

His father began to speak about politics, the corruption of the state, weakness of the current military leaders and how strong the army was back in his day. He was mad about the unwillingness of the soldiers nowadays to sacrifice their lives for their nation. Salah was nodding his head without understanding anything that his father was saying. Salah knew that his country was full of controversy. People are not easily pleased and they have been fighting for many decades. Any conversation with his father will lead to a dead end, as usual. He cares about his country though; yet, his mind was busy with something else. The various items were coming together for him, but Vivian was the main thing running in his head now. Finally, he asked for his father's permission and went to his room. He closed the door and climbed into bed.

For a couple of hours, he couldn't sleep; he kept thinking about what happened with Vivian. He had to be more mature and in control of his desires. He shouldn't have depended on her reluctance, although she didn't mind doing it, in the end, she looked like she was annoyed when she asked him to leave her alone and not to call her for a while.

He thought of several possibilities, but all these possibilities were unclear. He is now attracted to her more than ever and can't get her image out of his mind. He has a big decision to make in the coming days.

Crossroads

It has been almost a week after the incident. She never replied to his messages or answered the phone calls for the entire week. It wasn't that her phone was out of the coverage area all those days. He was sure that she was avoiding him because of what happened between them that day. Having sex with her was the most beautiful thing that had happened to him in all of his life. He didn't regret it. The taste was still in his mouth; taking her in his arms, fulfilling his lusts and satisfying his dreams.

She must be in shock, as is he. Until now, he doesn't understand how this happened. That day, everything went quick and easy. They did not have a chance to think about it rationally. Maybe if they had, they could have avoided it. He knew that if they got together, alone for a while, they would get into something intimate. That's what his ghost kept warning him about. Sometimes, things happen and there is no way that people can stop it, especially a beautiful thing like this. How would he be able to stop it?

He was dreaming about it, day and night. He feels bad and worried that Vivian is not answering him. But, at the same time, his strong wishes for her are strongly driving him. This makes him incapable of continuing his life without her. He is more connected to her now than before. So here he is now, heading to where she lives.

He decided to go and talk to her about it. She must know that he loves her now more than ever. For him, she is still the most pure girl he had ever met and he can't live without her anymore, especially after what happened that day. He is not going to lose her or lose this new world he found. Yes, he made his decision and he is going to tell her about it. She will be happy to hear that, because she joined him in his search and helped him to find his way. He will tell her that he made up his mind to become a Christian and he is ready to do anything it takes to be with her, even if he has to be baptized. Why should he wait? No need to waste more time. He saw God in a vision which happens only to a few people; those who are chosen by him. He went to the church and attended mass, where he met Christian priests, memorizing the main prayers. Except for the one called the Nicene Creed, he only remembers the first three words; it was too long and the font was incomprehensible. However, he can review it again and memorize the Creed. It won't be that hard for him to do so. Memorizing one page is something easy for a guy like him to do. He has read many books in his life and memorized tens of poems by famous poets.

He will tell her that, what happened between them was not a mistake. It was God's will for both of them. It's a sign. God wants them to be together. After being baptized, he would take her to a faraway place and marry her there, in an old, big church, with bright marble columns. They will be surrounded by dozens of white flowers, sacred incense will be filling the place and white doves will fly above their heads. The big organ will play all the beautiful songs the beautiful music will declare them husband and wife in front of God.

He reached the building where he met with her and Father Josef the first time. He rang the doorbell; this time firmly, full of confidence. The surprise wiped out all of his confidence when he saw father Josef answer the door instead of Vivian. He tried hard to control himself and not to go back on the reason he was there. So he greeted him and said "Hey... I mean, how are you Father Josef?" He was stammering" I am here to see..."

The priest interrupted him: "I know why you are here. Come in, let us sit and talk." He led him to the hall where they had met for the first time.

Like a meek lamb, he followed him, thinking to himself; perhaps this priest knows why he came and the reason behind his visit. Could Vivian have told him about what happened? His worries increased after he sat down, without hearing any signs of Vivian. It appeared they were alone. Only he and Father Josef were in the house.

Father Josef started with a question: "Are you here to ask for Vivian, after what happened between you?" This was so explicit for him; he never had a direct conversation before. He used to delay his opening statements before coming to the main point, especially regarding the subject they were talking about.

"Yes sir," he replied clearly and courageously. "I am here for Vivian," he said without hesitation. "As long as you were direct with me, I will be honest and tell you everything about Vivian and I. I had a lot of things going on in my life, for the short period of time after I met Vivian. Many changes happened to me and my way of life and I can tell you, I am now a new person."

"Dear Salah," the priest interrupted him again. "Let me be more honest with you. Vivian has told me everything about you, to include the new relationship between her and you. I advised her and I will also advise you. You need to know that things were strained for both of you. You two started off on the wrong foot, which ended up with inappropriate actions."

"She made a big mistake when, she took upon herself the task of helping and guiding build a relationship with God. Taking you to all these places was wrong, I advised her not to do so because she can't be the one to bear such responsibility. She should have passed it to other people, rather than doing it herself. This role was not meant for her. She was in a critical situation herself and the timing was not right. But as usual, she didn't listen to me. She has always been stubborn regarding her life events. She has been this way these past few years that I've known her."

"But our situation is different. We love each other" Salah replied.

The priest turned in his chair, exhaled deeply and said, "Please Salah, I want you to understand the situation correctly." He paused and glanced at the cross hanging on the wall with a look of sadness and regret. "It was my fault. I should have stopped her from meeting you. I should have been more firm with her. She has suffered a lot in her life. There have been many mistakes in her past and most of them were not her fault. She hasn't learned how to deal with people and how to understand the real world. Poor girl, life was so hard on her from the beginning and, the last bad thing that could happen to her was to know you and to be involved in all your matters; this has made her life more complicated. She was already starting to restore and rebuild some of it. Then you appeared at this time, as a new distraction, which affected her decision making process."

"Please Father; you don't know what Vivian means to me now. She helped me, giving all her time and, her love. She is the one who helped me navigate my search to find new life and become a good person."

"Look Salah, when you came here you were looking for God. So, my advice to you is, stay away from all the people who you were involved with in your life here and focus only on your relationship with Him. Nobody is more important than the main reason which drove you to be here, which was looking for God and doing his will in your life. Please forget about Vivian. She has her own plans now, which are far away different than yours. Please remember that you two belong to a different world. Obviously, your world is totally different than hers."

"We can fix this," Salah said with a tone of determination. "I will change. I can do whatever it takes to become like her. If you don't believe me, ask her and she will assure you that I am ready for that."

The priest replied in a firm tone, "This is over. It is too late now."

"What do you mean?"

"Vivian is gone now."

"Where is she? Where has she gone?"

"She has chosen her path finally. She has decided what is good for her and for her future"

Salah listened to him as he explained how she had joined a group of nuns. They are working with humanitarian and Christian efforts, to help the Christian and Yezidi refugees fleeing their cities and villages. The people are fleeing because of the fighting and attacks directed against them from the Islamic State Army in Mosul and other nearby areas controlled by them.

Father Josef tried his best to convince him that this was the best thing she could do for her life. Her choice this time was definitely right. It made her feel good and satisfied. She believed that serving others is the way to fulfill her calling, which is a noble calling. She was called to serve others, especially the needy people who are starving and suffering persecution.

Salah felt as if the ground was spinning after being stunned by this news. He asked him, "and what about me? I can't give up on her now."

"You must not be a stumbling block in her way; this is not a good time for you show back up again in her life. Please, listen to me. Forget her and keep going on with your own life. Go back to your family and people. Try to communicate with them again. Leave behind all that has happened to you in these past few months. Forget everything about Vivian and forget us also."

"No, I can't. It is too late for me now," Salah said in a trembling tone.

"Yes you can. You must do as I say. We can't afford to get into any more trouble than we are in now. As a Christian minority in this country, we are in the midst of the hardest time in our history, in this land. Lately, we have been persecuted, killed and displaced from our own cities and villages. Nobody can do anything about it now. No one can fix it, neither me nor you; not even the governmental army. It is over Salah, it is over," patting Salah's shoulder, nodding his head trying his best to persuade him. "You must submit. Not only for your sake, but for Vivian's, I know you love her and you will do what is good for her."

Concerning Father Josef, Vivian's decision was the perfect solution to all of her problems. Her life had been full of faults and unfruitful relationships. At least for the time being, she will be able to get away from all of this and avoid falling again, in another distorted relationship with someone; someone who is totally different from her, her religion and way of life. The next time, it would be a very hard fall. It could totally bring her down. More importantly, it was she who made this decision to leave and join the mission in the north. He encouraged her to do so. More than that, he was happy to have provided her with all the telephone numbers for the right people who can help her to reach her goal. He was so satisfied with himself, as he usually is, regardless if he was doing the wrong or right thing. He was protecting the Christian institution and all of its followers by keeping Vivian away from Salah.

Follow Your Heart

Salah left the place. He was unable to accept the outcome of the course of events. He wondered to himself, could this be the end? Is this the result he yearned for, after that long walk he took? Is this the end of all these beautiful new things he had gained? He is not capable of deciding what to do next. Should he smoke a cigarette and ask his ghost for guidance and what to do now? He doubted that the ghost will help or support him. He won't help him with his desires. He might advise him, just as the priest did. Yes! He will tell him not to go after Vivian and try to forget her forever.

But how can he forget her? How can he get her out of his head? He can't. She became part of his heart; she now flows within his blood, through his veins. No. He won't ask the ghost, or anyone else. He will listen to his heart and, his heart wants to be with her. He loves her too much. With her, he found what he was looking for and this time, he will hold on her tightly.

So, he decided to follow Vivian to where she was located. He will avoid asking Father John again about Vivian's location, because he doesn't trust him anymore. He might go to another priest, or ask some other people. He knows many Christians now, after spending a lot of time with them in all their activities and meetings, Thanks to Vivian, she had tried her best to introduce him to everybody.

First of all, he needs to go to Mosul. From there, he will start his search for her. Vivian was born in that city, which is big, beautiful and located in northern Iraq. He heard how it was populated by different groups and different religions.

The city is surrounded by green trees on all sides. There is a cool breeze at all times during the year. It is a city of old churches and historical monuments. If the city has been taken by the Islamic State, then it will be different now. He imagined it falling into darkness, controlled by criminal sectarian gangs. The Caliph and his followers say they want to enforce Sharia Law, but all they are doing is enforcing their bloody, violent law. Their goal is, establishing an Islamic Caliphate state all over the world and Mosul is just a starting place to launch this campaign.

How he hated those extremists, with their twisted talk and teachings about God, forcing others to do their will. They are supported by the sheiks and mullahs, whom in their speeches instigate a reign of terror by teaching hatred towards other people. They preach by shouting and yelling during their Friday sermons, threatening everybody with being burned in hell. They keep forcing people to practice their rules, first on their own families. They then want to spread this everywhere in the world, doing whatever it takes to accomplish this mission. If they have to kill and bomb innocent people, they will, just to apply their rules in this world. They hate everyone; Christians, Jews and they even hate Muslims if they are opposed them. Sometimes, they will hate themselves, even if they can't find someone to hate. They are rapists…criminals.

He stopped at this, thinking of Vivian being with those dangerous people, Surrounded by the Islamic State fighters in this city, she must be in grave danger inside the Dragons Throne.

"Oh, Vivian…Dear Vivian, how noble and such a delicate girl you are, going to this hell; to the most dangerous place on earth. It is a place from which everyone is trying to escape. You went there of your own free will, just to help and take care of others. How great you are! You make me hold on to thoughts of you more than ever!

"Behold my love, I am coming to get you out" he cried loudly, these were his last words, spoken with determination as he walked back home, ready to proceed with his decision.

A Flying Bird

He hastily prepared his luggage for travel, which usually was no more than a plastic bag filled with flip flops and a towel. He usually has to buy other items wherever he goes. He buys new underwear and socks, throwing the old ones in the garbage. His lifestyle was an exercise of his freedom. He learned these lifestyle characteristics by abstaining from things such as clothes and money. He used to do everything in its time. For example, he ate when he was hungry, smoked whenever he felt the need and flew like a bird wherever he wanted. The only thing in his life he couldn't overcome or control was to quit smoking.

He stepped out of his room with the bag in his hand. He went to where his father and mother usually sat in the living room, watching a drama series on television. He stood in the middle and announced to them, "I am going to the city of Mosul for a few days."

The father gazed at him saying, "What are you talking about? Haven't you heard what's happened in that city? There is a war going on now and people are being killed there. ISIS will kill you once you step inside the city."

He didn't care about what his father said. He had to go. This was his destiny. He replied with nonchalant shrug, "I will go anyway."

The mother started to cry and weep when she heard her son insisting on going.

All the noise brought the older brother Ali out of his room, wondering, "What is going on? What is the matter, Salah? And why are you holding a bag? Where are you going?"

The mother answered, "Dear Ali, you came in just in time. Your brother Salah wants to go to Mosul."

Ali said, "Really!? My brave brother! You are now my hero. You are going to fulfill the religious leaders calling and join the popular forces to defend the country against those terrorists from ISIS."

He looked at Ali in astonishment. For the first time in his life, he had never seen Ali so excited about something Salah was doing. Ali turned to the mother and said, "Mom, let him go. You can't prevent him from obeying the call of duty. Our great leaders, in their Fatwa, called all men who are capable of carrying a weapon to join the popular forces and defend the country. "

As the father sat silent without objecting, the mother resentfully said, "My son, what are you saying? Encouraging your younger brother to join the fight? We could lose him, as we lost your other brothers. You are pouring more gas on fire."

Ali replied to hear harshly, "You don't understand, so keep silent. You have no right to object to this calling. We all need to submit to the call of the Imam." The father grimaced. He was upset and rebuked him for the disrespect of his mother. Then they all started arguing and shouting about the situation. Salah stood there silent, between them, like an empty bucket. Their voices were pounding in his head. One thought was spinning in his head; he needs to travel as soon as possible. He has to find Vivian and bring her back before the war becomes worse. He could lose her forever. He can't waste time with them. He has already lost enough time with his family, as they have drowned him in darkness for a long time. He can't remain in darkness anymore. He must follow the light. So, he ran to the door, leaving his father and mother behind, even after all their attempts to keep him from leaving failed. Ali was shouting at them, "Leave him alone. Don't stand in his way and don't prevent him from doing this. He is now a real man." Catching up with Salah, Ali said, "Go to one of the Imam's main offices. They will tell you how to join the forces and reach the city, as all the main roads leading to the city are now closed."

Salah halted his steps, turned and said, "Do you mean that there is no way to reach the city?" For a moment, he had desperate thoughts. If the main roads are closed, how can he reach Vivian?

Ali answered, seeming very excited about this, "most of the people are taking a plane to the airport in Erbil, and from there they try to get a car to Mosul. But you won't need this; you just have to reach the imam's office, where they are recruiting men now." Salah was satisfied with this information. He left quickly, while the sound of Ali was echoing behind him, "I will pray for you, Allah will give you victory over his enemies."

For the first time in his life, Ali is pleading for him to defeat the enemies. He no longer knows who the real enemy is now. They are everywhere, sometimes among his family and people. He wished that he had time to tell Ali that he doesn't want to die; that he is in love and hangs on to life more than ever. He wished he could tell him about the new God he knew. But time was running out for him. He needs to reach Vivian before getting lost in all of the conflict.

At the end of the street, he stopped a taxi, got into it and ordered the driver: "Get me to the closest travel agency. I need to get a flight."

Catch the Dream

He couldn't believe that he had paid two hundred and fifty dollars, just for a short, one-way trip from Baghdad to Erbil. Nonetheless, he was ready to spend every cent he had, just to get there. Erbil is in the north, 62 miles east of Mosul; he could get a ride from there to where Vivian is located now. This was his plan, plus a side mission. Some people in Baghdad asked him to deliver money donations to a priest there. His name is Father Fady, He will go to the church first and deliver the money, an easy and simple plan to be accomplished.

It was overcrowded at the airport; a lot of people were standing in many lines, waiting for their flights. Obviously, all the main roads connecting Baghdad to most northern cities, like Erbil and Mosul, were closed or abandoned. When the Islamic state's fighters take over a road, they plant different kinds of bombs and mines, preventing military movements Therefore, travelling on overland routes has become very dangerous.

Once he stepped onto the airplane, he was irritated. Inside of plane was a mess and many people started pushing him to move forward. Nevertheless, he paused in the middle of the aisle, looking at his ticket and trying to find his seat number. Choosing a place to sit was always something important to him, even if it was on a plane. Beside the window, near the tail or at the front, he was guessing. Suddenly and in a harsh voice, someone from behind shouted, "What is going on there? Please move on! Can't you just sit down? We are stuck here."

He stumbled then moved on. He was uncertain of his decision, looking at each seat closely, until he saw a priest he had met before with Vivian. It was astonishing to him; how many priests are involved in this quest until now. He greeted him and said, "Hello Father, how are you?"

"Hello," the man glanced up, unable to identify him.

"Don't you remember me? I am Salah. I came to your class with Vivian."

"Oh…yes my son. I remember you."

"Can I sit beside you?"

"Sure, come on, sit down. At least we can chat together during the trip."

"Thanks."

"You're welcome. Why are you traveling to Erbil? Do you have relatives there?" The priest wondered.

He stammered for a while, thinking of a suitable answer that won't draw suspicion to him. "I…I am on a mission, I am carrying money for the priests in Mosul, for the displaced people."

"Oh, that's a noble thing for you to do. But unfortunately, you are too late my son."

"What do you mean?"

"Two days ago, ISIS fighters threatened all Christians in the city and nearby villages. This caused all the people to run away as ISIS forces approached them. They are all now heading to Erbil as it is the only safe place."

This news was almost powerful enough to knock him down. His mission became more difficult now. At the beginning, he knew where to go. He was going to where the nun's mission was located. Vivian had joined them, as Father Josef said. But now, how can he find her in this mess? Where will he start his search? This mission was rapidly becoming a search for a needle in a haystack. He fell into despair.

"I can help you if you want," the said priest offering.

"Really?" His face shone with hope, "that would be a great if you could help me."

"I know where all the priests fleeing from Mosul are gathering now, I know the place they are seeking refuge with the people. I can take you there. It's at the main archbishopric in Erbil."

"Thank you. I would be very grateful."

At this offer from the priest, he rested assured. At least he now knows where to start his search for her. During the flight, many questions were running through his head. Where could Vivian be now? Is she helping the refugees in these places or still in the city with the people who stayed behind? A terrifying thought of Vivian being kidnapped or killed by ISIS came over him like a heavy black cloud. It could be the end of the world for him. If that probability is real, then he has lost her forever. There will be no way to bring her back. All these questions, mixed with his fears, started spinning in his head like a heavy storm until he became tired and exhausted. So, he laid his head back on the seat and relaxed. As usual, to run away from his fears, he closed his eyes and imagined the big church, with its long marble columns, shining bright like glass. The sacred altar in front of him was covered with doves. Peace, like a cloud, was covering the place, all the while fire and war were waging, surrounding the building on all sides. But, he felt safe and fully protected there. From these images, Vivian emerged in a white, shiny dress and landed slowly. It was like she was an angel, come down from the sky to save his soul. She stepped toward to him and put her hand on his head. What a wonderful feeling. Her magical touch refreshed and revived him. Her touch was more charming than having sex with her, much more. It was like the touch of a loving mother to her baby. She hugged him and sat beside him. Then a high pitched voice shouted, jolting him saying, "Come on Salah. Get up. We have arrived."

Lost People

Long hours passed without smoking as he sat in the rear seat of the car. They were on their way with the priest to the archbishopric in Erbil. In the front, the priest sat beside the driver. The driver was telling different stories about what had happened to the people when ISIS attacked them. They were sad and painful stories, almost incredible. After a while, he asked the priest for permission to smoke. He began explaining his desire to help people. "Yes Father," he said to the priest, "I've walked this long distance to be with all of you and to provide any kind of help."

"That's a good thing to do my son" the priest nodded. "You seem to be a noble man. As you see, the situation is very difficult. Indeed, we need all the support we can get."

"Well, I am here to join you."

"Everyone in this country has to realize the critical situation we Christians are facing, especially as a minority. Minorities usually feel weak, so when they face real danger or a threat, they are easily affected. They start looking for other countries to emigrate to. So, that's why they need any kind of protection they can get."

"Of course my dear Father. I know this, and for this I came here. I am ready for this mission. This money I have must reach those who need it." He was smiling and feeling very proud as he said, "I am happy because at last, I have a role to play, a true message to perform in my life." He relaxed, bending his back on the seat. Inhaling deeply from his cigarette, he blew the smoke out. Looking forward, he became awestruck, unaware of the smoke cloud clearing away from his sight. The face of his ghost was in the mirror above the driver, smiling in a wicked way.

He was startled because of him. "You again!?" Resentful, he asked him, "Why are you smiling thus? I know the meaning of your smile. But this time, you are mistaken."

The ghost replied laughing, "No, I'm not mistaken. Behold, you have missed things again."

"Nothing is missed. Everything is in the right place," Salah replied firmly.

"I'll ask you a question so, answer me honestly. For what purpose are you walking this long and crooked distance? Do you really want to help people?"

"Yes, I want to help people. I have nothing to hide."

"Maybe that old religious man believed you. But as for me, I don't buy it. You are here because you want to find Vivian and these people are the only way you can get to her. Why don't you tell them the truth? Confess that you are here seeking her and all that you told the priest is just lies."

"No, this isn't true," Salah replied justifying his deeds. "Ok, let's say it is true. So what? I'm looking for her, to be a part of her mission and the work she is doing. I am changed now; I want to help others reach their goals. At least for one time in my life, I want to do noble and good deeds."

The smoke ghost answered, "There is no reason to prevent you from doing that. But, you can't deny the great hunger you have for Vivian's touch, your deep passion for her warm hug, a kiss from her lusty lips. This is your real reason; you are keen to fulfill your own needs. Don't try to cover it up by some noble and supreme principles; it is your real reason," he cited regretfully. "You human beings, as usual, make it personal, just for your own benefit. Then, you write slogans and use colorful words to cover up. But inside, you are worse than you seem and pretend to be. You just cater to your own needs, lusts, desires and nothing more."

Salah tried to get rid of this annoying ghost; get him out of his head. So, he opened the car window to get the smoke as far away as possible. He was taken by the scene he saw when he looked outside to the streets. People were everywhere, filling all the places. In the gardens, the public squares and the big buildings. For the first time in his life, he observed something terrible. Thousands of people were without homes, living in tents and lying in the streets. Many of them were old people and children, suffering outside in the hot, dry weather; heated by the sun.

He could hardly believe what he saw. All of these people were displaced by ISIS. How could they do that? What evil will is driving ISIS fighters, with their Caliph who is leading them like a black dragon? With his beasts, swallowing hundreds of cities and villages, sending to ash every child and women he sees in his way. He has a thirst for blood and a longing to kill, driving these nationals out of their homes and taking their beautiful cities, which were yesterday thriving with life. Today, the cities have become full of darkness and black clothed gunmen. How could people treat each other this way; carrying all that oppression in their heart. Does hatred and evil towards humanity go to that extent? Perhaps the smoke ghost was right in everything he said about him; when he accused him and all humans of being bad creatures.

They arrived at the building and got out of the taxi. On their way to the main door, the crowds were around, filling the place. The priest said to Salah, "Stay with me, so as not to be lost; until we arrive at the main door to the archbishopric; the crowd is heavy. If you get lost, you won't be able to get in."

Salah followed him as they quickened their pace, passing through the people. Some of them were sleeping on the ground, others were jammed together. Reaching the door was a difficult task for them. They had to force their way through the crowds. Accidentally, he stepped on a child's hand with his full weight. He felt her flesh and small bone, as if it was a piece of dough under his heavy foot. He stopped and looked down to see the child's face. She was a very young girl, smiling in a strange way.

She smiled! He had stepped on her tiny, soft hand with all of his weight, causing her terrible pain. Had it been him, he wouldn't have been able to tolerate it. He didn't understand. Why had she smiled when he stepped on her small hand? How could she smile and not cry? Perhaps she was hungry and had lost her sense of feeling; maybe she couldn't recognize pain and didn't know how to let it out. Sometimes when a human loses his humanity, he loses his senses too. His natural reactions and feelings are not expressed. He cries instead of laughing and laughs when he should cry. This is how people adapt and cope in such brutal conditions. It was also the result of long years of hostility, with many decades full of war, fighting and endless conflicts. It became impossible for people to remain normal, or to be like other people in other places. A nation is like a seed which has to grow and become a big plant. To grow correctly, it needs pure air, fertile soil, and care. These people hadn't received such treatment. They never got an honest farmer to take care of them. A good farmer usually works hard with his hands in the field. Therefore, he is sure of the harvest, because he sowed the seeds, worked hard and took great care of the plants. A good farmer is not like a thief who comes in the time of harvest only. They jump over the fence to steal from the ripe crops that they didn't plant. This is what happened to these poor people. There were many decades of war and fighting, years full of carelessness, selfishness and individual interests. These activities lead to a regrettable result.

He followed his escorts until they reached the main gate. There where people standing there, knocking at the door with their hands and feet shouting, "We want a solution. Find us a place to stay." The priest stood with Salah by the door, waiting for it to be opened. One of the protesters glared at him and harshly said, "Tell them that we can't wait anymore. If they won't protect us, we will leave. We will find another country to live in." He stood fast in his place, while the men surrounded him, staring angrily. He wasn't bold enough to look in their eyes. But, he felt the disappointment and desperation coming out like steam from their noses. He could barely hold himself, trying not to melt by the hot exhalation coming out of the boiling chest of the men.

Moments of waiting passed, as if they were ages. Finally, the door was opened and he went inside. The big hall was full of religious men; a lot of priests and leaders from different churches.

Ongoing dialogue between them was about the conspiracy against Christianity in Iraq. There was talk of a global Masonic movement, jointly with big western countries and other local parties, for the purpose of destroying the local church and ridding the Middle East of traditional Christians. Despite all this talk, he couldn't understand what they meant. Everybody was talking yet; he was just listening and greeting whoever passed him by.

People were very busy with the meetings. The event was so serious, because of its impact on the nation, the fate of this country and their existence. The country, to which they belonged for thousands of years, had become a catastrophe. A janitor approached him and asked, "I have been sent by your escort. What can I do for you?"

He told him that he had to deliver an important message to someone in charge here. The man asked him to have a seat and wait. He sat on a chair beside a man who was middle aged and seemed to be waiting for something. The man poked him with a finger. He looked at him wondering and said, "Yes?"

The man said, "What do you think?"

"What do I think? Of what?" he replied.

"Of all the church leaders? Of the meetings here? Do you think they can achieve something good? Do you think they can solve this situation and help people with their own tragedy?"

"I don't know," he thought for a while then cited, "Why not? They are leaders of the churches. They must have many ways and a strong will to save their own people."

"You are an optimist!" the man said mocking, then added, "I don't think they can do anything. Do you know why?" he paused for some time, waiting for Salah to respond.

Salah asked, "Why?"

"I'll tell you why," he said, shaking his head. "They are not meeting for the same goal and they are not united as one voice. Each one of them is driven by his own denomination. They are obeying regulations, not God. They don't want to concede to each other. Just like politics, they are politicians too, sometimes worse than that. You will see. My words are correct. Just wait and you will see."

After some time, a priest came towards them and asked Salah, "Are you Salah, who came from Baghdad?"

"Yes sir." Salah stood up.

"I'm Father Fady" stretching his hand to greet him. " They called me from Baghdad and told me about you. Thanks for coming all that way, just to help."

"You are welcome Father. I have this money that I need to give to you; some of your friends sent it." Before he handed the money to Father Fady, another priest arrived with the Janitor who asked him to wait.

"Just a moment Father Fady," The priest with the janitor interrupted, said, "This man has to deliver the money he carries to me."

"But, the money was sent in my name, from people whom I know and I am the responsible for it," said Father Fady opposing.

"No. You are under my authority here. Everything coming in here must be under my control. This man was looking for the person in charge here and that is me. Moreover, you don't have any authority in this region. You are out of your diocese limits." Salah was watching them as they were arguing. Unwilling to be a part of their fight, especially during this critical time, he didn't say a word. But, he was surprised to see priests fight for power and money.

The man who was sitting beside him dragged him back to the chair and said, "I told you that my words are correct. These leaders can't solve anything; there is no hope for us.

Anyway, give them the money. You have done what was required from you. Go and find a safe place for your family."

"I have no family here," he said, "I came today from Baghdad; I want to help with this suffering, which is going on now. But, I don't know where to start and where to go."

"I see you are a good man with true intent to help. Go to the camps, on the main road west, outside Erbil, I overheard the nuns talking about a lot of people in these camps. That is where all the volunteers and helpers are going. The situation is terrible there."

Salah's eyes glimmered with hope when he heard this. Maybe Vivian joined one of these camps. Although, searching for her between these places and among all these people will be very hard. He turned around and put the money in the hands of both priests, who were still arguing. He turned to the people in that hall, for trying to find out about the camps and how he can get there. Then, he set out to find his way to the first camp. He will search every camp, determined to find her, even if he has to look at the faces of all the people, one by one.

Three Days in Empty Circles

The smell of mold and the stifling humidity emanated from everywhere, making it difficult to breathe normal in this building. That was the feeling the first moment he entered the place. It was a refugee camp, known to the people as the 6th Service Center. This center was a big building with three stories, occupied by displaced people after they had lost their homes when ISIS invaded their cities. This is the sixth refugee camp he had entered in his quest for Vivian over the past three days. Each time he reached a camp, he was thinking it would be the last one. But he found nothing there and had to go on.

While he stood in the middle of the big yard in front of the building, everyone started staring at him. Then they stepped out toward him, one after another, until he was surrounded by a bunch of people. Frightened by them, he stood still, unwilling to move and unable to figure out what was going on. They asked him a lot of questions, trying to find who he was. He answered them cautiously.

After learning who he was, they all turned around and left him alone. He realized then that they thought he was one of the international organizations' employees who used to come here, providing help; some of them came with food assistance and other stuff. The other type of workers the people were eager to meet was the United Nations employees, who wrote down the refugee's names and information to get them out of here to safety. At least that was what all of them were hoping; to get any kind of help from any visitor.

After being left alone, he sat down on the floor beside the walkway. He looked closely at the building, examining it. The waste water was covering large parts of the big yard, forming a dirty pond full of green moss and covered with bugs. Obviously, this place was meant to be a big school, because it has a lot of halls and rooms. But it was abandoned for some reason. No one had been here in a long time. The walls were full of cracks, corroded and sticky because of the high moisture. The floors were in bad condition as well, full of holes. The color of the tiles had changed over time. This place was not fit for human habitation. By all means, it was a disaster. But for the displaced that have no home, it was better than sleeping outdoors.

He started thinking about himself and checking the results of his quest. He has been searching for three days. He had run out of money and has no place to go. He was left with no choice but to stay for a while in this place, though it looked like hell. He will rest and sleep for the night, regain some strength then, proceed tomorrow morning. He was bored and had become fatigued of searching and asking everybody whom he meets about the camps. But, he was still hopeful about the possibility of finding something that leads him to Vivian's location.

It was almost afternoon when a deep desire drove him to smoke a cigarette. As soon as the smoke appeared, his ghost was in front of him with his grim face, berating Salah he said, "Haven't I told you before? Don't pretend that you have forgotten."

Salah carelessly said, "I am so tired of trying to remember things you have said to me before."

"I told you...In this life, you will not get all of what you desire. Look, your journey has had many holes. For three days, you didn't sleep well. You've spent all your money. You didn't even have a shower or wash your face and you didn't touch a clean bed or eat a full meal. Until now, you have nothing, not a single clue that can lead you to Vivian's place. What are you waiting for? Can't you see?"

"I see nothing in front of me."

"The truth is in front of you, but you can't see it! Do you know why? You don't want to see it. You only want to see what your heart desires. But now, here in all this despair, it is sneaking like a thief into your heart, driving out all love and the dreams you hoped for yourself."

With a look of sadness, Salah said, "You know, in spite of my wish that you could be wrong with what you said, your words seem true. I'm tired and I don't think I can continue another day. I need to rest."

The ghost replied, "Exactly, that's what I'm trying to show you."

"You are right my dear ghost," Salah said acknowledging.

The ghost of smoke smiled and said proudly, "As usual, I'm right, and you are wrong."

"Well, I wish you wouldn't look at it that way." Salah replied disturbed.

"How do you want me to see it then? When you are wrong, you say: Things were not going in my favor, or you say: The situation was too difficult for me, and you keep bringing up similar reasons to convince yourself it was not your fault, that it has nothing to do with your nature of weakness and inability. On the other hand, when things go well with you, you say: This was accomplished because of my wisdom, my supernatural thoughts and my brave actions. Isn't that right?"

Salah replied: "You can say whatever you want. I don't care now who wins the debate. I'm tired, starving and I have no desire to discuss all of this with you."

"Don't be so desperate. Look ahead; you don't know what is coming," The ghost said.

Suddenly, strange movements occurred in this dreary place. Dozens of people started to crawl out from the rooms and the tents installed in the buildings yards. Gradually, they filled the area of the front square. This made him wonder, where have all these people been hiding? Were they piled on top of each other or maybe, they were kept underground? People started gathering in the square in the hot burning sun. After hundreds of them had filled the place, they started lining up, forming circles, leaving an empty space in the middle and a long path, two and a half meters wide. Salah was watching all this with wonder. What's happening? What kind of strange power drives all these people? It's as if they have been trained in this process previously, over and over. They performed perfectly, as if they were a dance team, or an army squad. There were more than a thousand people in that space. How could they be so organized? Acting like one man. Suddenly, everyone stopped moving. A profound silence came over the crowd, like someone dropped a needle; they will hear its sound. All at once, everyone turned their heads, looking in one direction. It was as if they were all expecting something important to come towards them from that direction. It was like watching a movie in the theater.

Soon thereafter, a truck entered the area, carrying pots of food and a lot of plastic containers. Even from a distance, the smell of food in the truck filled the place. When it reached his nose, the smell stopped him in his tracks; he was very hungry. Precisely at that moment, he realized that the ghost of hunger is subjecting this crowd to his will. They had learned how to move regularly, all the while waiting for the food; sincerely obeying the orders and memorizing the steps. He saw how great the power of this ghost was; mightily effective on the conduct of human beings and making them obedient to such a degree. They follow the signs and learn the lessons very well, like mice in cages, or hens in domestication pens. Truly, human beings are well trained animals.

The truck stopped in the middle of the crowd; in the void that people prepared earlier. A team of workers on the truck started giving out plastic food packages and bread to the people surrounding them. Due to his severe hunger, he penetrated the crowd to get some food. It was not easy to reach the truck, but he did his best to get there.

For a moment, as he approached the truck, he saw the face he was looking for. It was Vivian, on the truck distributing food. Finally, God responded to his prayers and there she is; he found her! He lunged with all his might to grab the truck and started shouting at her: "Vivian, Vivian, I'm Salah". But the voices of the people were louder than his. So, he jumped on the side of the truck and kept calling. However, she didn't hear him; she was busy working with her colleagues on the truck. Suddenly, the truck started moving. He stayed by it then, climbed on its side. He jumped inside the truck and shouted, "Vivian, Vivian I am Salah, I came to see you". When Vivian saw him and realized that it was him, she turned around and reached out to greet him. That moment meant everything to him. He was ready to give his whole life for this moment. He stepped forward to her, clutching his hands around her waist. He embraced her tightly, pulling her to his chest. He wanted to squeeze her in his arms so hard that she couldn't leave him again. He kept repeating, like an echo, "Vivian, I love you, I love you, and I love you." This big happy surprise and the way he climbed the truck consumed his remaining strength. He was hungry and hadn't eaten for the past few days. It had wiped him out, so he fell unconscious into her arms.

Unreachable Mirage

The next morning, he woke up early, trying to remember the details of what happened the previous day. He really was too tired and powerless last night, so much so that he slept without being aware of what happened next after he held Vivian in his arms. Instantly, he realized that sleeping after finding Vivian is an improper idea yet, he had to see her. He rushed out of the tent looking. It shocked him, once he stepped out and saw all the tents that had been erected during the night while he was sleeping. Who did all that work!? Erecting hundreds of tents requires an army of trained workers. The number of displaced people who entered this place was unbelievable. They all came in during the night, seeking a refuge. He noticed his partner in the tent, sitting on the ground, nodding for him to come over. It seems that he did not sleep all night. The man said to him, "Finally you got up. You were so tired and sick. We had to bring a doctor to see you. Do not be afraid my friend, you are okay now. You just needed some sleep and a vitamin injection."

Salah asked the young man, "How long I have been sleeping?"

"Twelve long hours." The man pointed to the ground, inviting him to join. "Come, sit down and have a bite. You will need it. It is early morning and we still have a long day of work. A lot of people will be coming to this camp in the next few hours. We need to be prepared. God is with us. Don't be afraid."

He sat with him on the ground, quietly having his breakfast. He glanced at him, unable to keep from asking the question, and then said, "Where is Vivian now?"

"Vivian…She went with the team to buy food from the market. They need to feed thousands of hungry people today." He paused, sighed and then said, "Yeah, she works hard. I don't know how we could manage all that work without her, God bless that girl."

"Do you know when she will be back?"

"Normally, they take a long time, but she will be back by noon. I assure you of that," the man answered with a broad smile on his face. "You need to get more rest."

Waiting until noon was not easy for Salah. Therefore, he decided to wander around the camp until Vivian came back. He walked to the camp gate, which was near the main road. This is where all the people would arrive, walking for long hours in the dry, hot weather. This weather made him feel bad. He was still felt weak, so he stopped to take a breath and watch the civilians arrive. They were coming in by the hundreds, some by car and others were walking. Watching them made him wonder, what did these people do to deserve what had happened to them? Why had they encountered such a cruel fate?

Meanwhile, a group of people walking by came close to where he was standing. There were women, men and old people, but no children. Although they had arrived safely at the camp, they would turn their heads occasionally, looking behind them, as they were making sure there was nobody after them. Like panicked prey running away from the hunting beasts, they rushed to the tents as they approached them.

They looked awful, with their torn cloths and dirty faces, covered with dust. Like ghosts, they were all reflecting one color, the color of death. Some of them were whining, others were silently walking. He imagined how he would look like if he was evicted, if he had lost his house, possessions and savings. What would he do if he was forced to flee his city, barely clothed and nothing else? It was difficult for him to accept such a fate. Walking slowly, this group of refugees passed by him, staring at his face; he looked at their eyes. He couldn't say if they were even human beings. Their eyes were empty, devoid of any feelings. It was like he was looking into an animal's eye. It was the first time in his life he'd seen eyes like this. This was strange and terrifying to him. Eyes are the reflection of the soul; the inner human mirror that reflects what is inside. But, through these people's eyes, he saw dead bodies with no souls. It's obvious now how human beings could become animals, due to all the pain, brutal beatings and hunger. This was too much injustice for them to endure. How can people treat each other with such cruelty? Human beings were created to be like God. They were commanded to take care of each other; the strong helps the weak. But instead, they are killing each other and the strong eats the weak, like animals. Could this be the real fate for humanity?

He immediately remembered his ghost's words again. He was right in everything he has said about a human's desire and his willingness for destruction, for the sake of his purpose. Salah kept watching the people passing by him. One by one, without being able to move out of their way or at least turn his back to them, he didn't know why he stood still there. It felt as if his feet were nailed to the ground. People were passing silently past him; glancing his way then continuing to walk. Suddenly, one of the women came very close to him. She started to scream in a strange way.

He felt the scream came out of her bowels; torn from her insides, almost strangling her voice. She started whimpering for a while, and then cried, "My baby, my baby. Give me back my baby," She threw herself to the ground and caught his feet, pulling his trousers and crying "please, bring back my baby to me. They took it from me. They promised to bring it back again, but they didn't. Please sir, if she wakes up and doesn't see me beside her, she will be afraid and start crying. She is now hungry and needs me to feed her. I'm ready to do so," She stood up, opened her shirt, took out her breast and held it in her hands pointing it towards him. She then started squeezing it, like she was feeding a child and said," I am ready for her, can't you see? I have milk and she is hungry. I want my baby back." The sight of this woman, holding her breast in her hands while shouting and screaming was a terrible sight for him. It was very hard for this mother, her baby taken away from her. She has lost her mind. She became crazy.

People gathered around the woman. They put some clothes on her upper body. She fainted and fell down.

The event she had experienced was too hard to be endured. Therefore, she collapsed, overcome with grief. He could no longer stand here after observing this. He turned around and started running to his tent. He ran as fast as he could, unwilling to watch this scene anymore; he was seeking a safe place to hide himself away from this woman's face and from anyone else in this camp. He ran faster and faster, escaping the bitter reality of this world, He was running away from all the bad things surrounding him; running from the crushing injustice and oppression. He was running from all the pain these poor bodies had endured. He ran away from the unjustified silence of God. God's indifference towards the rampant evil all over this world is taking away everything good and replacing it with destruction.

He entered his tent, sat down on the ground. Burying his head in his hands, he started weeping like a baby. He continued to cry for a long time. He had saved his tears for this worldwide tragedy and now, it's his chance to let it all out. He cried torrential tears, as if he was crying for the loss of his grandfather. He loved him and wished that he had stayed with him longer. He was crying for his mother and father and for being away from them all this time. He was crying to God, whom he had discovered recently. He loved God passionately. But, he is drifting away from him again, taking all that peace and safety he has acquired for the first time in his life. He cried because he knew Vivian and her new world. His heart was touched; his life was changed by this God, when he breathed the scent coming out from the altar in that church. It was mixed with his grandfather's smell, emanating from his old cloak that is saturated with the smell of old tobacco. He was crying for Vivian, the beautiful girl whom he is seeking. He is running after her desperately, as if he was after an unreachable mirage. Vivian is the love he dreamed about all his life and still, he is unable to hold that love in his hands.

It is too much pain for him to carry on his own. He closed his eyes, exhausted, trying to stop all these images that are appearing in his mind's eye. To stop this onslaught of images that is like a storm inside of him now, he laid his head on his arms and fell into a deep sleep.

The Good Shepherd

A soft, gentle hand touched his shoulder, waking him up from his sleep. Lifting his head, he was barely able to open his eyes. It was Vivian's face. She was looking at him, with her great smile which made him feel happy.

With a voice full of tenderness, she said: "You slept again. It sounds like you were very tired. Are you feeling better now?"

"Finally, you are back," holding her hands. He kissed them like he was making sure that she is real and not a ghost. He gripped her hands strongly so she wouldn't leave and disappear again.

She pulled her hands from him gently and said, "I am here. Don't be afraid; everything is going to be alright."

He said, "Please Vivian, don't leave me again, I…"

She interrupted him, "we are all here now with you." She gave him a warm smile. "We finished the work outside; all of the people have had their food and have a place to sleep for tonight. How about you? How was your day?"

"I went for a walk, among the tents and I saw the situation of the people."

"Did you see the tragedy," she was indignant. "Did you feel the pain?"

"Yes, I saw everything, and I wished I hadn't. It's much harder than I imagined. How can these people withstand all of this injustice? It's too heavy for any human being to bear. And this is too much for you Vivian. You can't stay here anymore. That's why I came, to take you back with me; you must forget all of this."

"What? Go back with you?! "She became edgy, "Where I go? And how could I forget all of this? No, it's too late, I can't go back now."

"But I need you." He put his hands on her shoulders.

"And people here need me more than you," turning her face away.

"But, I love you Vivian," he said trying to look into her eyes. "Please Vivian, I love you." He was sure that she was ready to respond to him as before, when she did a lot of things for him.

"Salah! Please! You must forget what happened between us. It was just a one-time thing. It passed away at the same day it happened."

"Forget?!... Me?! I can't! I can't forget you now. I found my life with you. You are everything to me."

"And I found another meaning for my life." She looked him in the eye, very determined and serious.

"What is it? Is there another man in your life?"

"Another man!" she giggled then, paused for a while. Sighing deeply with relief she said, "I found something else; better than any man. I found that my place is here…right now at this particular time, there is a big need for me to help, right here where people are suffering."

"What?" Unable to understand a word, he said, "But, what about us? What about the new life we discovered together? What about all of our conversations about faith and how a man must do his best to find his path in this world, without paying any attention for another, or even care for what they want from him. We agreed to be different from the people around us. We agreed to find our life's calling. You taught me all of that. Only with you, I found a meaning for my life and I was able to hold the truth in my hands. I want to be with you forever." He paused and shook his head rejecting, "I can't accept what you are saying. I strongly refuse to accept your decision," looking at her with tearful eyes. "Please Vivian, please think of me. Are you willing to leave me? After all, you are the reason for my deliverance. You showed me the way to the truth. It was you who saved my soul. You enlightened my heart. Through you, I knew God in a different way. You brought me to this point. If you abandon me now, I will fall. I will be lost again. I can't... I can't live without you." He put his head in her lap and started crying like a baby, begging his mother not to leave him alone.

"Oh... Dear Salah, not all of what you said is true. Likewise, not all that we want in life we can have," she said with shedding tears. "You are driven by your emotions. What you have now is just a fleeting feeling. It will pass very soon. What happened between us was make-believe, and I mean not only by you, but by me also. It was not meant for our relationship to reach that point." She let out a sigh of regret and continued talking, "all of the events went too fast for me, and I lost control at some point; because everything around me was unclear. I was holding on by seriously seeking for something with meaning; to add it to my life. I was looking for a sign to help me decide where to go. You appeared to me when I was at the crossroads. My relationship with you helped me to understand myself more than before and recognize my path." She smiled that beautiful, charming smile like she used to, "I enjoyed the time we had together. It was the most beautiful experience I have ever had in all of my life. Salah, you were the greatest thing that ever happened to me but, good things always come late. For uncertain reasons, this leaves us regretful for all the happiness we couldn't grasp. Now we have run out of time. It's over now. You can't share your future with me; I'm on a different path now. It's a difficult mission and must be fulfilled. You have nothing to do with all of this. I was not ready for you or for anyone else. My life was too complicated, full of problems and bumps. I am a broken woman, who can't join with any man in his life. I need to rebuild myself first. This is my destiny, I found it finally and I am happy with what I have found; this will help me to make my life better."

She breathed deeply, stood up and walked a few steps to the tent door. Looking forward at the people outside, she said, "Salah, I can't give you what you want. I've made my mind. Nothing can change that." She turned to him pointing, "Can't you see? Can't you feel how big the tragedy is here? Those are my own people. They lost their homes, their women and the young girls have been kidnaped and raped. Some of them were killed and tortured." She turned back again, looking at the people, "This nation of mine developed over thousands of years. It's the nation that invented things and taught people how to read and write. Now they have become refugees. They have lost everything and no one will take them. I must stand up for them. I must provide help and support in this critical time. This is my final word, I will dedicate myself to the service here, to help and protect their existence and fate. I came to this decision after a long time of prayer."

"I asked God for a sign to lead me, and here is the sign. It's there," she said pointing to the outside. "It's in front of me now. Look carefully. Thousands of fleeing, homeless people; they need someone to take care of them and protect them until this situation is over."

She stepped towards him, sat down beside him, looked him in the eye and said, "I want you to think about what you said. Don't be dragged in by your desires only. Don't run away from facing the world again; I am not the solution to your problems. Pursue your call to God. He is the purpose you started this trip for from the beginning. Get yourself a better life. You are really a special person and I will be praying for you always."

She touched his cheek with her palm softly, smiled at him and said, "I remember when I saw you the first time, when you came to the church. I felt as if there was something special and honest about you; you had a pure will for knowing God, without any purpose or deformation. I admired your strength and courage; you've got something different from the others. The people I knew around me were just sheep that follow the flock. You've got the will to get out of your environment and to set yourself free from all the boundaries in your community. That is what makes you a real human being, who is close to God and knows him, deeper than others. It doesn't matter if you were born Christian or not, or how long you have been following God. Very few people in history could do something like you did. That is why you are unlike others, because of your enlightened heart. You have a seeking soul, which gives you all this strength. Unlike other people, you are a pure man, not stained by human dust. You are still carrying the color of the angels, which disappeared a long time ago from this dark world in which we are living."

Without a word, he was looking in her eyes while she was talking. He knew that every word she said was right. He was thinking how ironic it is, that all the surrounding circumstances came together now and are acting against his will? But, can't it be different than this? Is there any possibility to change what is going around him now? A miracle or something from the sky could suddenly decide to interfere and stop the war. End this fighting and killing. Burn all of those ISIS fighters with their Caliph and stop all of this now; for a little while. Maybe Vivian would listen to him and agree to what he wants. She could change her mind, respond to him and love him again as she did before.

But it would be like howling at the moon if something like this happens. The world doesn't run like this; never giving us our desires to easy. That's what his ghost used to say. Yet, the opposite is what usually happens. Life opens wide the door for us, just to show us how great and beautiful what is kept behind the doors. Then life closes the door while we are still outside. It's as if God is telling us: "everything is there; love, happiness and your sweet dreams. But you are not going to hold it in your hands." He often wondered why it has to be like this. What is the wisdom of God when he doesn't give us what we want in full?

He can't imagine his life without Vivian. It would be a hard life, tasteless and meaningless. He wondered about the purpose of all he had experienced and lived in the past months. Was it fake? Was it only a waste of time? He can't start over again without her. He felt like a baby abandoned by his mother. The picture popped up in front of him. It was the image of the crying woman, holding her breast in her hands. Her eyes were empty of any meaning or feeling, except for the pain. Her face had the color of dust. He could taste the bitterness of her sight. Then she stopped crying and started laughing loudly. Her shaggy hair was dirty and full of bugs. Opposite of this woman's situation; he found his stand; he stands odd, weird and empty of feelings towards the people and their misery. He is just thinking of himself and his interests by asking Vivian to betray her persecuted people, giving up the noble call she finally found for her life. She cares for others and their needs, and he just thinks about himself, pushing her away from her good work for his own needs. How selfish of him to think only about himself.

She interrupted his thoughts, "Salah, listen to me, I think we need to start evacuating this camp."

"What?" as he was awakened from a deep sleep, "Why?"

"Because it is the closest camp; close to where ISIS is approaching now. They control all of the villages around us, and they are pushing their fighters towards here. It won't be long time until they reach this place. That's what they have told me today. You saw the large number of people who came here this morning, running from the brutality of this organization. With all the numbers of children and women we have here, that make us the favorite target now. "

He looked at her wondering what she meant by this.

She explained saying, "That's what ISIS does. They recruit the children and sell the women and young girls for sexual intercourse. Don't be surprised. That's what the Islamic state is all about, money and sex. It is all in the history haven't you read it? Anyway, we can't stay here forever. The evacuation will start tomorrow. I will stay here to help who is going to stay behind, waiting for their family members to arrive"

"No, we need to complete our talk," he said holding her hands.

"Salah, we don't have time to talk now. The army will arrive here to secure the region and stop ISIS advancing to the big city. This place will become a battlefield. Shooting and fighting will be everywhere." She looked at him firmly and said, "Do as I am telling you."

For the last time, he wanted to ask her. Maybe she would change her mind if he started begging her." Vivian, please… Vivian listen to me, for the last time, I beg you, come back with me, I…"

Suddenly, a loud sound boomed; the sound of a rocket as it hit the camp. They both trembled and left the tent; the scene in front of them was terrifying. Bombs were falling from the sky, hitting the tents and the people. Some of them were injured. Everyone started running, trying to get out of the buildings and the surrounding tents. Chaos took over the place. He and Vivian started running while she kept calling him, "Salah stay with me." He ran, joining in with the people around him, turning around to make sure that he won't lose Vivian in the middle of this crowd. She kept close to him. Finally, she grabbed his hand, dragging him out of the way. Leading him to the side road, a speeding car launched and parked near her, as she was pointing and shouting to the driver. She opened the door and said to him, "Let's go! Don't look back!" He was happy that they were together, holding her hand. So, he did what she asked him. She pushed him inside the car and closed the door. She smiled and said, "Go, and don't stop until you get home. You can create a new life for yourself. Love God and love other people" He clung to her hand and said, "What about you? Aren't you coming with us?" She slipped her hand from his and gently held his face in her hands and kissed him on his forehead, then commanded the driver to go. The car went fast amid all this confusion; he was shocked by Vivian's sacrifice. Giving of herself for others in that way. Only a true shepherd will do this. She had become a different person, much stronger than she was before. Indeed, Vivian has changed and found the real path for herself.

Emmanuel

After two hours, the driver stopped at a military check point which belongs to government authorities. They waited for their turn to be checked in before entering the city. The process seems like it will take a long time, due to the long queues of cars and people. Everybody was trying to enter the city, after ISIS fighters attacked their territories. He watched the crowds that filled all the surrounding roads, awaiting their turn in the lines. People were using different kinds of vehicles; small and big, buses and trucks. Some of them were riding animals. He saw people being isolated from others, for screening and security concerns. There were many groups of different humanitarian organizations, listing the people and providing food and emergency supplies.

Some people were allowed to enter the city. Those who had no relatives or sponsors were kept in the tents near the check point, which was already overflowing. Food and water was running out very fast. He was very sad to see all of these people in the open air, in the sun, facing hunger and thirst and waiting without any sign of help for them. They had no other choice but to wait. The car in which he was riding passed the check point without any noticeable problems. The driver went directly to the archbishopric to drop Salah and others there.

Everyone got out of the car, including him. They all entered the front yard of the building, which was overcrowded. He edged his way through the people who were gathered together on the grounds. He joined them, taking a small spot for himself, nothing underneath him but the grass. Besides his hunger and being tired, he was still in shock. He was in shock because of the result he ended up with, after the long trip, carrying within him all those high expectations. Now, all his dreams and big hopes have faded. None of them will ever come true. He couldn't believe what happened. Losing Vivian is the bitter truth that he has to accept. He wondered if he was wrong in the way he thought about his quest from the beginning. Was it possible that he missed some signs which he had not taken into consideration? Or, he may have followed the wrong signs that made him delude himself with unreal truth. But, where was his ghost? That wise companion, why didn't he warn him? Why didn't he advise him in a good way, so he could follow the right path? Many of the questions were left unanswered inside him. A driven need to talk with someone nagged at him. Maybe he could get suitable answers telling someone what happened in the last few months. He thought of his ghost. Nevertheless, he had no interest to call him or talk with him. It's better for him to be alone for now.

The sun was dropping, heading towards dusk. Darkness was covering the big square and the garden, occupied by the displaced people. Most of them were on the ground sleeping, using blankets, paper boxes, or anything that can be used as a mattress. He tried to stretch, but he barely had enough space in his spot, jammed between others. The grounds were crowded, more than it could handle. He sat cross-legged, incapable of closing his eyes. He looked around with a feeling of discomfort at all of these bodies around him. There was no roof above his head, just the sky. Gradually, the stars started to light the night sky. Absence of the moon made the darkness very heavy. For the first time during this trip, he was afraid and worried to be among strange people. They made him feel that he was a homeless, just like them. He remembered that he also had no house to go to now. His family was far away. They don't know anything about him, especially over the last days. They might believe he is dead by now. He was hungry, feeling cold, sad and desperate. Suddenly, as he was looking forward, a slow movement came out of the darkness; an old lady was standing in front of him. She wasn't there earlier. She appeared suddenly, as if she came from a hidden world. The old lady turned her head to the left, then to the right, looking at the sleeping bodies, as if she was a mother checking on her children. After a while, she stepped towards him, with heavy steps. She could barely stand up straight due to the bend in her back. He was terrified, as she was getting closer to him in the dark.

He couldn't take his eyes off of her. She stopped three feet from him and lit a candle. Then she bent over, enough to reach the ground and put the candle in front of him. He was carefully watching everything she was doing. Then, the light of the candle revealed her. He saw her face, white, and full of intertwined wrinkles, enriched by life experience of her long years. She looked at him and smiled, then declared in slow calm voice, "So much need for prayer at this time."

Once the candle was lit, its light opened the darkness around him, transferring the big, dark gloomy yard into a bright domestic place, imposing silence on everybody. The spreading light and the full silence expanded around, like ripples spreading in the water from a falling stone. These ripples of light were starting to become bigger and bigger. They covered the whole yard, the building, the streets nearby and then into the entire city. The light was everywhere, as if the night turned to midday and silence took over. It was as if everyone was in silent prayer. He was in the middle, surrounded by all these people who were pleading for him.

The old lady was staring at him with her white face, which seemed familiar. She was like someone he had known for a long time. Yes, the face was not anonymous to him; her eyes were glistening by the candle's light, in this dark night. They looked the same as his grandpa's eyes, when he used to talk to him as he was going to bed. The eyes were assuring and encouraging him not to be afraid of the dark and to stop crying. For nothing is worthy, compared to his precious tears. Losing things doesn't mean that it is the end of the world. Yes, he understands his grandpa's message now. Everything in this life can be restored. There is always a way. Nothing is determined. Despite the fact that he lost Vivian's love, he is accompanied now by the love of this unknown lady. He is surrounded by thousands of people, though they were all strangers, they were praying for him, prompting him to stand up and go on in his life. Everything now was working for him, supporting his call in a great way.

He felt like time had slowed and the earth had stopped moving. Just like the people, the events and this life. Everything stopped for him, to give him a chance to go back to himself and hold onto it. A great feeling of comfort and assurance emerged him, the same feeling he had the first time he saw Vivian. That was when he felt God's real existence and got to know him in a different way.

He felt a special love overwhelming him now; and through all of these people around him. He closed his eyes on this beautiful scene, laid his body down, sharing the ground with the others and fell into a deep sleep.

Return...and not yet

Early in the morning, he was awakened by loud voices. It was breakfast time and many young volunteers were in the yard handing out food to the people. He stood still unwilling to move from his place, waiting for the food. The picture of the old lady with her white face was stuck in his mind. Her elderly face, made him remember his mother. He searched his bag for the cell phone; he had forgotten about it over the previous days. He didn't talk to anyone, or send a message telling his family where he was located. They must be anxious about him. He held the phone in his hand, searching the names list. Looking for his mother's number made him realize how much he missed her and needed her love. It's time for him to go a home now.

Returning to Baghdad was not easy, because he had to buy a plane ticket. All of the roads between cities were still closed because of the fighting between ISIS and the army, backed by the popular forces. He was in a hopeless situation. He had no money to pay for the flight. After many attempts, he managed to talk with Father Fady, the priest whom he met the first day when he arrived at the archbishopric. He explained to him what happened during the last days. How ISIS attacked the camp, how he ran from the bombing and had to take the car with the other survivors until he arrived here at the archbishopric. The priest sympathized with him and with his need to go back home. So, he bought him a plane ticket to Baghdad and took care of him until the departure date.

During the days while he waited for his flight, Salah didn't ask too much about what happened to Vivian and the other people in that camp. The terrible pictures of the people were not easy to wipe from his memory. But, he heard from Father Fady and the driver that all of the people were deployed to another camp. Vivian was still with them and taking care of them. That was all he had to know; he was satisfied with it.

The return trip was long. He spent two days traveling, between flights and taxis to and from different places. Besides, there was the intense checking and scanning he had to go through because of the security concerns. It was afternoon, when he finally arrived at his neighborhood. He was so excited to meet his mother, to hold her in his arms and inhale her scent. He was also anxious to see his father's face and kiss his hand. However, when he reached the corner where the tea kiosk located, he looked around him. It was incredible to be back again. He stopped and sighed, deeply inhaling. The smell of tea penetrated to his nose. The smile was irresistible; he had missed it a lot. So, he was thinking that his trip has ended and he has safely arrived home, which was only a few steps away. His father and mother are probably sitting in the house now, watching the TV series. They seldom go out at this time of the day, so, no harm if he has a cup of tea.

He threw his bag on the ground and sat on one of the plastic chairs that were placed on the sidewalk for the customers to use. He ordered a cup of tea and lit his cigarette. When he exhaled the smoke around him, his entire life started playing in front of him like a movie, from the beginning through to the recent events of the last few months. It was a special trip, an extraordinary one which was full of hard, heroic and powerful events. It shook his being and made him a different person, much different than before, stronger and sure-footed. This trip was not for Vivian. It was for his sake, in order to understand himself better and to find his path. He knew that a man has to be free of all boundaries and limits that he puts upon himself. He must be liberated from what the community puts on him. He is responsible for his freedom, because the decision to be free lies in his hands.

He is the one who can break all that calcification that was formed around him over time. He has to get rid of all kinds of stagnation; mentally, socially, and spiritually, that has been forced on him. This has captured him and turned him into a creature with no soul.

Now he knows that there are no differences between various beginnings, which a man can choose and make in his life. The most important thing is to take it honestly and do not doubt his own starting point and his own path, which became part of his life. He must be content with the answer he gets when he asks a question, whereas the adventure is within the question itself. He has to enjoy the question more than the answer. The question carries within itself a beautiful secret that keeps it alive, peculiar and remains spectacular forever.

He finished the cigarette, still waiting and wondering. Why hadn't the ghost appeared? Could he have gone and left him? Or, maybe he doesn't want to talk to him anymore? Anyway, he doesn't need him now, because he spared all the answers. He is now capable of understanding life better than before and understanding everything around him, without the help of anybody. He was satisfied with all the results that he had reached in his mind and heart. He was happy with all of it. All of that made him feel reassured and rested. Ultimately, the primary goal of his quest was to get inner-peace for his life.

Quietly and very slowly, he extinguished the cigarette in the ashtray, looking pensively at it. A calm smile came over his face, as if he was saying goodbye to it. He paid Ghanim for the tea. Ghanim is the worker who said, as usual, complimenting, "Don't worry about it. It's on me, Mr. Salah. We missed you; come again."

He got up from the chair and grabbed his plastic bag. He walked slowly, a few steps on the sidewalk then, stopped there, looking at the horizon, up at the buildings. Sunset was different this time. The sun turned a dark red color. He had never seen such a sight before. He took the cell phone out of his pocket, pushed the call button and waited a few seconds. His mom answered and said; with the affectionate sound he was eager to hear, "Hello." Now he was certain that everything is over. He is back for sure. He put the phone near his mouth," Mom, its Salah. I am back."

She burst into tears, crying: "Salah, my dear son! Where are you now? I was dying... to know… about you. I... I..."

He hardly could understand her: "I am ok mom. I am back. I am here. I love you Mom; please stop crying."

"I love you too, dear." She tried to take a breath, "we missed you! Please come back now!"

He controlled himself, giving her some time to calm down and then asked her: "Where is dad?"

"He is at the mosque, offering condolences to one of our neighbors. He will be back soon. Salah, don't be late. I will be waiting for you--" Suddenly, there was a big explosion in the area. An enormous gust of air came from behind him, throwing him up in the air. He fell sharply to the ground, dropping the cell phone out of his hand and the bag too.

For few minutes, he didn't feel his body and could hardly open his eyes. He was lying on the ground between the chairs. The view in front of him was foggy; a deep, heavy whirring sound in his ears prevented him from hearing anything of what was going around him. He tried his best to stand to his feet, staggering as he tried to stand. He checked his body to make sure he was not injured. He felt dizzy, but he was lucky to be uninjured. People around him were running in a state of panic, shouting, "a suicide bomber blew himself up at the mosque." Gathering his thoughts together quickly, trying to remember what happened: the mosque … offering condolences… his father. He ran to the mosque quickly, passing through the people. Some of them were running away from the explosion, while others were trying to help the injured. He jostled with the crowd, who were gathering at the place. He could barely make way to get to the building's gate. Half of its upper parts fell to the ground and the other parts were smashed everywhere. He crossed the front yard, which was full of dead bodies; others were injured and shouting. He looked carefully among them, but he couldn't find his dad. He went inside the big hall where the people were offering their condolences.

Dust filled the place and falling rubble from the building covered everything, making it difficult to identify the bodies on the ground. He saw from a distance, the body of his father lying on the ground. Once he approached him, he realized that he was dead. His entire body was covered with dust and blood was flowing out of his chest.

He sat down on the ground, holding his father's body in his arms. He pulled his dad's head to his chest and started crying. He lifted up his head and looked at his face. His eyes were closed and dust covered his hair. His dad's face was calm, despite the big, devastating explosion that broke everything in this place. He died with no pain, quickly and very easy. A big piece of shrapnel went through his chest then, into the heart and killed him on the spot. He was praying when this happened.

Salah looked around the place; it made him remember the church he saw for the first time. A deep calm ruled the place. White dust was scattered everywhere. Like a scent, it covered all the parts of the hall. It looked the same. He couldn't see clearly, but the altar was in its place as usual, at the end of the hall. A white building block fell to the ground. It looked like the statue of the Virgin Mary with her white dress, which he had seen once before in the church. Cracks covered the walls all around. A broken picture of Imam Hussein reminded him of the icon of the chained man on the cross, with blood flowing from his side.

The calm face of his dead father was exactly like the face of his grandpa. It reminded him of Vivian's beautiful angelic face, with all her calm and innocence. At that moment, he saw God's face in his father, as well as in his grandpa and Vivian. They all had the same face. He felt God, still with him and loving him…. He felt his real existence, breathed deeply and repeated:

> *"We believe in one God*
> *The father almighty*
> *Maker of heaven and earth*
> *And of all things*
> *Visible and invisible*
> *And in one…" and he continued…*